Tracking Daddy Down

J

K

Tracking Daddy Down

Marybeth Kelsey

Greenwillow Books
An Imprint of HarperCollinsPublishers

Tracking Daddy Down
Copyright © 2008 by Marybeth Kelsey

The text of this book is set in Centaur.
Book design by Victoria Jamieson

Library of Congress Cataloging-in-Publication Data

Kelsey, Marybeth.
Tracking Daddy down / by Marybeth Kelsey.
p. cm.
"Greenwillow Books."
Summary: Daredevil eleven-year-old Billie has an exciting summer, in spite of her overprotective stepfather, when she figures out where her father and uncle are hiding after robbing a bank and enlists her cousin's help in convincing them to surrender.
ISBN 978-0-06-128842-5 (trade bdg.)
ISBN 978-0-06-128841-8 (lib. bdg.)
[1. Fathers and daughters—Fiction. 2. Stepfathers—Fiction. 3. Cousins—Fiction. 4. Family life—Indiana—Fiction. 5. Robbers and outlaws—Fiction. 6. Indiana—Fiction.] I. Title.
PZ7.K302Trc 2008   [Fic]—dc22   2008003828

First Edition 10 9 8 7 6 5 4 3 2 1

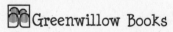 Greenwillow Books

‖‖‖‖‖‖‖‖‖‖‖‖‖‖‖‖‖‖‖‖

For my husband, Terry Walter, and sons,
Christopher Murrell, Eric Murrell, and
Max Walter

For my aunt, Ann B. Haithcock

And in memory of my parents,
Kathleen and Bill Kelsey

‖‖‖‖‖‖‖‖‖‖‖‖‖‖‖‖‖‖‖‖

Tracking Daddy Down

Chapter 1

The summer I turned eleven, my daddy, Earl Leon Wisher, took a gun and robbed the Henderson County Bank in Millerstown, Indiana.

He did it in broad daylight with his older brother, Warren, and from what I heard, they never even bothered to disguise themselves. All they did was tie checkered bandannas over their mouths, so of course they were recognized right off.

"Morons." That's what Mama said the day we heard the news. "Dumb as doorknobs—both of them."

I didn't say anything at the time, but I figured Daddy wasn't as dumb as she claimed, because word had it him and Uncle Warren tore out of Millerstown that day with more than ten thousand dollars. And nobody had a clue where they ran off to, either. Nobody except me, that is, and I sure didn't have any plans to squeal on my own daddy. I'd already lost him once, back when I was in third grade and he took off for California, leaving both us girls with Mama. I wasn't ready to lose him a second time.

I heard about the bank robbery on a Wednesday in June, right before my eleventh birthday.

The day started out normal enough. I'd been out riding bikes around our town of Myron, Indiana, with my best friend, Ernestine, and my cousin, Tommy—he's Uncle Warren's boy. We decided to stop and play a round of double dare on South Street Hill. For riding bikes, South Street was the best—smooth and steep.

It was my turn to make up the dare, so I gripped the middle of my handlebars, balanced my feet on the back fender, then wove from one side of the road to the other all the way down the hill. The faster I got going, the more my eyes bugged out with excitement. When I hit bottom, I jumped off my bike and sent it spinning to the grass. I lay panting on the side of the street, waiting for Tommy and Ernestine to follow my dare. But neither of them moved. They just stood at the top of the hill, like they were glued to the pavement.

"I ain't doing it," Tommy hollered. "My chain's too rusty. It might come off."

"Liar," I yelled back. "You're a sissy."

I knew that would get him. Tommy acted tough, but when it came down to it, he never worked up the nerve to do half the stuff I did. Not that I'm bragging or anything. Mama always said I was reckless, that I didn't act like I had the sense God gave a chicken.

"It'll be a miracle if you don't kill yourself with one of those daredevil stunts," she'd told me.

I glanced up to see Ernestine whizzing straight down the middle of the street, her tangled red hair blowing around her face, her mouth working furiously on a wad of gum. She skidded for several feet before stopping. A pang of envy stung me when I looked at her new red bike with its padded seat and slick chrome fenders. Her rich aunt Myrtle from Washington, D.C., had just bought it for her.

"Chicken," I said when she stopped.

"Am not."

"Are too. You didn't even ride the fender."

Ernestine spit on her handlebars and wiped them to a shine with the bottom of her blouse. "That's because my bike ain't broke in good enough yet. I can't take any chances on it. My aunt Myrtle made me promise."

"Can I ride it?" I'd been eyeing that bike for a whole week, but so far she hadn't let me or Tommy so much as sit on it. She claimed we might dent the fenders.

"Myrtle says no, not till I've had it a month." She fidgeted with the red, white, and blue streamers hanging from her handlebars.

"Well, it doesn't matter anyway," I said, acting like I didn't care. "Daddy's getting me a new bike for my birthday. He says I can pick out whatever one I want."

Ernestine's eyes widened big as Tootsie Roll Pops. "For real? I thought he didn't have any money."

I guess I could understand why she'd think that, seeing as how Daddy hadn't ever bought us kids anything except for a piece of candy now and then. Mama said he didn't have money because he couldn't hold a job. But ever since he'd come back three months ago, Daddy had been working steady at Ray's Auto Parts over in Millerstown. Plus, he'd told me about the good job he'd had out in California and how they still owed him a bunch of money. He said he'd be getting it any day.

"What do you want, baby?" Daddy had asked me a few days ago, when I'd reminded him my birthday was coming up. "You want one of those big Kimmy dolls they got in the window at Clarksons'?"

"Daddy, I don't want a doll. I want a new bike, one that has streamers coming out of the handlebars—like Ernestine's. Only I want a blue one."

"No problem. You want a bike; you'll get a bike," he'd promised. "Soon as I get the money owed me. I'll buy the Kimmy doll for your sister's birthday."

That would make Carla happy, for sure. She was only five, and she'd been begging for a Kimmy doll ever since we first saw them at Clarksons' Five and Dime in downtown Myron. I couldn't have cared less about the stupid thing. Mama said I'd always been a tomboy—which is why she called me Billie instead of Billieanne—and that I'd never played with dolls, even when I was little. All I knew was that Ernestine and I had lots more fun tromping along the railroad tracks or playing dodgeball with Tommy than we did brushing some doll's hair. I didn't blame Daddy for not knowing any of this, though. He'd been gone almost three years, and I figured he'd just forgotten the things I liked to do.

My thoughts were interrupted by a "Whoop!" Tommy came flying down the street straight at us, both arms high above his head, his front tire wobbling like it wanted to fall off. He did some kind of tricky fishtail, bumped over the curb, then ended up smack in the middle of Mirabelle Hudson's flower bed.

I cringed. He couldn't have picked a worse place to crash. I happened to know those purple gladiolas were Mirabelle's personal favorites. She did all the flower arrangements at our Myron Methodist Church, which sat right next door to her house, and I'd heard her tell the preacher's wife how she always saved the purple gladiolas for special occasions like weddings and church banquets.

I also knew firsthand about Mirabelle's fiery temper, seeing as how she'd baby-sat us kids so much. We'd only quit going to her house a few weeks ago, after Mama married my stepdad, Joe Hughes. He'd said there wasn't any need for Mirabelle anymore since he usually worked second or third shift and was home to watch us kids during the summer days. If it had been up to me, I wouldn't have had any baby-sitter, and that's exactly what I'd told Mama.

"I don't like the way he watches over me like a hawk," I'd said. "He makes me come home a hundred times a day to check in. And he makes us eat stupid stuff for lunch, like tuna fish salad with celery, before we get dessert. It's not fair. Tommy doesn't have to have a baby-sitter anymore. Besides, I'm old enough to take care of Carla by myself."

"Is that all?" Mama had said, after she'd stopped laughing.

"No." I was on a roll by then. "He's been hogging my chair ever since he moved in here, he always gets both drumsticks when you fry chicken, and he hardly ever says a word to me except 'Where are you going?' and 'You need to be home in half an hour.' Besides that, he likes Carla better than he likes me."

Of course, Mama stood right up for him. "That's not true, Billie. Joe's a good, fair man. He cares for you both, and he's doing his best to watch out for you. Just give him a chance."

I'd decided she could talk him up until she was blue in the face, but it still didn't mean I had to like him. And I didn't like the way she had me and Carla call him Daddy Joe, either. Mama said it showed him respect, but so far the only thing I cared to show Joe Hughes was the door.

Tommy hopped up from the flower bed and brushed himself off. "Dang! I told you my chain was rusted. It came off when I tried to brake. The darn handlebars are loose, too. I couldn't even steer." He stared at his mangled bike lying in the middle of the flower bed.

The Hudsons' screen door flew open, and Mirabelle blew outside like a wicked storm cloud. She pointed her big beak of a nose in our direction.

"Uh-oh!" Ernestine scrambled behind me. She squashed herself up against my back, hissing in my ear. "Ohmygosh! She's going to kill us. I know it. She's going to kill us."

Mirabelle clutched the front of her tattered house robe and huffed and puffed her short, squat body to where we stood by the flower bed. Once she got a good look at the damage, her face swelled way up and turned the color of a beet.

"We're real sorry, Mirabelle," I said as fast as the words would spill out. "Tommy's chain came off, just like that." I snapped my fingers for emphasis. "It was an accident, wasn't it, Tommy?"

He stood speechless, his face pale as cream, his skinny legs quivering. I figured he must've been thinking about Mirabelle's five-pound paddle, which hung on a hook by her front door. Him and I had been at the wrong end of it plenty.

"Wasn't it an accident, Tommy?" I said louder, kicking his ankle.

"Uh . . . yeah . . . my darn chain slipped and then I got going up around thirty or so and I couldn't steer no more 'cause my handlebars came loose and I—I—"

Mirabelle snorted. "An accident? That weren't no accident, boy! That there was vandalism. I've a good mind to git my paddle. Look here what you kids have done. Them's my best bunch of glads."

She lunged forward, swatting at us with her hand. "Git! Git, now. Git on home. And don't you think I ain't tellin' your daddy Joe about this mess, young lady. He'll take a paddle to all of you."

We grabbed our bikes and pushed them down the sidewalk, since Tommy's wasn't fit to ride anymore. Once we rounded the church corner I peered over my shoulder, relieved to see that Mirabelle wasn't following us. I knew we hadn't heard the last of this gladiola incident, though. Mirabelle was sure to tell her husband, Whitey, who was also our Sunday school teacher and Daddy Joe's uncle. Whitey would see to it we got some kind of punishment—probably a month of daily Bible study with him as the teacher.

I wished Daddy wasn't living in Millerstown with Tommy's dad, Uncle Warren. It was five miles away. If only I could get to him quick and explain what'd happened, he'd smooth things over with Whitey. Daddy always had been a good talker; even Mama admitted that.

We stopped in front of the church. Tommy turned his bike upside down on its handlebars, and the three of us were hovered over it, working to fit the chain back on, when Ernestine sucked in her breath so hard I thought she'd swallowed her gum.

She grabbed my elbow. "Psst! Ohmygosh, Billie! Don't look now, but here comes your stepdad. For real. We're going to be in big trouble if he sees Mirabelle."

Shoot! My stomach rumbled with dread as Daddy Joe's station wagon eased up the road toward us. What did he want anyway? Was I in trouble for not reporting home on time? Maybe he'd already seen Mirabelle and believed her story of how we'd vandalized the flower bed. He might even have her paddle.

I kept my head down like I was busy studying the bike chain, but I watched from the corner of my eye as the car rolled to a stop. Daddy Joe cut the engine and sat there for a moment, looking at us from the open car window. I held my breath, wishing he'd sing out something bright and cheery to break the silence, something my real daddy would've yelled, like "Hey! It's mighty hot. You kids want to go downtown for an ice-cream cone?" Daddy Joe didn't, though. He just sat there, his mouth set in a frown, studying the three of us like we were pieces to some tricky jigsaw puzzle he couldn't figure out.

"Oh, man. He looks mad. We're in for it now," Tommy muttered.

I busied myself with the chain again. "He can go jump in a lake for all I care," I said as the car door opened.

Chapter 2

"**Billie.**"

Daddy Joe's deep, gruff voice froze my lungs so tight I could hardly catch my breath.

I don't know why he shook me up like that; he'd never laid a hand on me or Carla. He'd never even yelled that much, except to tell us to hush up when he was trying to sleep. In fact, Daddy Joe was so quiet I could never tell what was on his mind or if he was having a good time.

Maybe that was the problem. My real daddy liked to goof off and joke around with me and Carla, even on the mornings when he was too tired to get up. He'd let us jump on the bed and throw pillows at him, until he'd finally bury himself under the blankets and say, "I give! You girls go get your breakfast now, so I can catch a couple more winks here."

Those mornings with Daddy always seemed to make

Mama mad, especially the time Carla threw her pillow so hard it knocked a bottle of gardenia perfume off the dresser.

Mama had already yelled three times that morning for Daddy to get up. She'd come back to the bedroom to yell at him for the fourth time, I guess, right as the bottle crashed to the floor and spilled.

"Phew!" Daddy said, disappearing under the blankets. "That's some mighty powerful perfume. Somebody better clean that mess up before your mama sees it."

"I'm looking at it now," she'd said in a tight voice from the bedroom door. "I also see you're still in bed, which means you're going to be late for work the second time this week. How long do you think they're going to put up with that?"

"Aw, come on, Wanda," Daddy said from under the blankets. "Lighten up. It's no big deal. I'll stay later this afternoon to make up the time. Besides, I'm spending time with the kids, like you're always after me to do. We're having a good time, ain't that right, girls?"

I'd had to agree with him. And since Daddy said he'd make up the work time, I didn't see why Mama raised such a stink about his getting up a few minutes late.

She'd stormed back down the hall, yelling over her shoulder, "If you'd get home at a decent hour, we wouldn't have this problem in the mornings."

Daddy popped his head out from under the covers and grinned at us. "Your mama could use a better sense of humor. You think I should run down to Clarksons' today and buy her one?" He'd started tickling me and Carla then, until both of us were howling with laughter.

But Daddy Joe never tried to make us laugh. He wasn't a jokester, that's for sure. His idea of a good time was tinkering inside a broken toaster, or reading about ancient Egyptian pyramids in the *National Geographic*, or talking to Mama about all the boring news going on around the world. And whenever he had to get up in the morning, he'd set the alarm clock and hop right out of bed, no nonsense. Mama never once yelled at him to "Get out of bed and get to work," like she did my real daddy.

Daddy Joe pushed the car door the rest of the way open and swung his long legs out to the ground. I guess he was the tallest man I'd ever seen, way over six feet, and his hands were the size of Ping-Pong paddles. He looked at his watch. "You know the rules. You were supposed to check in an hour ago."

Ernestine stuffed a string of gum back in her mouth, then hopped up and snatched her bike from where she'd rested it against a tree. "Uh . . . I'd better get home now. I've got to help clean the house." She looked at me and rolled her eyes back at Daddy Joe. My chest tightened as I watched her sail down the street, her shiny fenders glittering in the sunlight.

Daddy Joe ambled over to us. "I've been looking everywhere for you, Billie. Your mom wants you at the diner. You go with her, Tommy. Better get on down there pretty quick now, both of you."

"What for?" From where we squatted on the ground he towered over us taller than a telephone pole. I barely worked up the nerve to look at him. "We're trying to fix Tommy's bike. The chain came off. Besides, I ain't supposed to work today—I worked yesterday."

Daddy Joe stared forever at me through his dark, deep-set eyes. I wondered how he could go so long without blinking.

"Never mind that. Just do as I say, please." He reached over and picked up Tommy's bike like it didn't weigh any more than a twig. "I'll get the chain back on this later today. Looks like the handlebars need to be tightened, too." Tommy and I watched in silence as he wedged the bike into the back of the station wagon. He gave us one last look over his shoulder before pulling away.

Once the car turned the corner I got up and spit after it. "Dumb turd! I hate his stupid guts. Ever since Mama married him, he's been telling me what to do. He ain't even my real dad."

"Yeah. He acts like he's big stuff, like he's the boss of me, too," Tommy said.

I yanked my bike up from the sidewalk, wondering why Mama had ever married that guy. It's not like she had any trouble getting men to notice her. In fact, it seemed like every man who came into the diner tried to flirt with her, so why did she have to go and pick the very worst one? If I'd had my way about the whole thing, she wouldn't have chosen any of them. Mama never bothered to check with me, though. She'd just up and married Joe Hughes two months ago, right after my real daddy came back from California.

"What do you think your mom wants? You think we're in trouble?" Tommy said as we headed across the street.

I shrugged my shoulders like I didn't care, but little seeds of worry sprung up in my mind. Had Mirabelle already called her about the gladiolas?

Since neither of us was in a rush to find ourselves in trouble, we decided to take the long way and follow the railroad tracks downtown to Wanda's Diner—that's Mama's restaurant. She'd worked there ever since I could remember; then, right after she married Daddy Joe, he surprised her and bought the place.

It's not that Daddy Joe was rich; he was just a supervisor at the Firestone tire plant in Millerstown. But Mama always bragged about how smart he was with money, how he'd worked hard and saved over the years—"Unlike some people I know, who blow through cash like it's dish suds," she'd told Tommy's mom, my aunt Charlene.

After Daddy Joe bought the diner, the very first thing he did was tear down the old MYRON RESTAURANT sign and hang a new one that said WANDA'S DINER. That sealed the deal for him as far as Mama was concerned. She started acting like he was the neatest thing since instant mashed potatoes, and all her attention went to him and the diner. She hardly had any time left for me or Carla.

Once, after my real daddy had come back from California and Mama was complaining about him being irresponsible, I'd said, "At least he comes around to see if Carla and I want to do something fun every once in a while. That's more than you do. All you ever care about is that dumb—"

"Go to your room right now, young lady," Mama had said. "And you can stay there for an hour. I hear any more sass like that from you, you'll stay back there for the rest of the day."

I'd just opened my mouth to tell her I was sorry when Daddy Joe cut right in and said, "I'd appreciate you not talking to your mother like that. Enough said."

"What business is it of yours?" I'd muttered on my way down the hallway. "You're not even a part of this family."

I was still fuming about Joe Hughes as I shoved my bike over the loose railroad rocks. Tommy raced on down the tracks, but I followed the sweet scent of honeysuckle into some nearby bushes. I stopped to pick raspberries, stuffing handfuls of the plump, juicy berries in my mouth. As my eyes followed the tracks into the horizon, I thought about all the times we kids had sat by the railroad watching the train rumble by, waiting for the man in the caboose to stick his head out the window and toss us some candy.

For as long as I could remember those train tracks had been a big part of my life. Tommy, Ernestine, and I had explored them so many times we knew every inch of railroad from downtown Myron all the way to the deserted glass factory about a half mile out of town. At night I'd lie in bed and listen to the lonely whistle of the train, imagining I was on it, heading out to California, where Daddy had moved.

Once I got my fill of berries, I picked my bike up and started back over the tracks. By now Tommy had sped way ahead of me. I saw him stooped over the ground, sorting through a mound of stones.

"Look," he said when I caught up to him. "This here's a genuine arrowhead." He showed me a small gray rock with a sharp point on one end.

I turned it over in my hand. "What else you got?"

He pulled a couple more stones out of his pocket. One of them was rust-colored and sparkly. "This one here looks valuable. I might be able to sell it."

I nodded in agreement, but I didn't really know anything

about rocks. Tommy did, though. He was an expert. He had books about them and a whole collection of rocks on the floor of his room, all stacked in piles marked "valuable," "medium-priced," and "cheap." He'd been selling railroad rocks door to door ever since we were little kids. I figured he was trying to make extra money because Aunt Charlene and him were so poor. Mama said they had even less money than we did, which I knew wasn't much. My uncle Warren had left them several years ago and moved to Millerstown; he hardly ever came around to help out anymore. And even when he did show up, it's not like he gave them money or anything. All he did was yell and stomp around and fight with Aunt Charlene.

Tommy stuffed the rocks back in his pocket and ran his hand through his short, sandy hair. When he grinned at me, it struck me I could've been looking in a mirror. We were the same age, the same size, and with our blue eyes and freckled faces, we looked so much alike some people thought we must be twins. We even had the same gap between our two front teeth.

I pushed my bike away from the tracks onto Main Street. "Come on. I'll give you a ride," I said.

He climbed onto my handlebars, and we headed down-town, swerving around the few cars parked along the street. There wasn't much to Myron: a grain elevator, the Polar Meat Locker, Dick's Grocery, the Myron Funeral Parlor, and Clarksons' Five and Dime. If you wanted fun, you had to go to Millerstown, where Daddy lived with Uncle Warren. That's where all the good stuff was, like the Millers Park swimming pool and Rocky's Roller Rink.

"Stop!" Tommy yelled when we got to Clarksons'. "Let's go in. I got ten cents." I'd started to worry a little more about what Mama wanted, but the thought of candy led me to follow Tommy right through Clarksons' door. Mrs. Clarkson was fussing with something in the dry goods section, while Mr. Clarkson had himself planted up front behind the candy counter. He watched us like a buz-zard, acting all worried we'd stick something in our pock-ets without paying for it. I'd never swiped anything in my whole life, but Mr. Clarkson wouldn't have believed me, even if I told him. He didn't trust any of us Wisher kids, and he didn't mind saying so.

"You kids got money? This here candy ain't free." Tommy pulled out his dime and showed Mr. Clarkson.

We picked out two Turkish taffy sticks, paid him, then left the store sucking on our candy. After crossing Main Street, we passed a row of gray-haired men sitting on the bench outside Fuzzy's Tavern and Pool Hall, right next door to Mama's diner.

"Your daddy Joe find you?" Fuzzy Hilton asked when Tommy and I walked by. I glanced back at him. I didn't know Fuzzy's age, but I figured he had to be somewhere close to a hundred. His face looked as wrinkled as a dried-up prune. A stubble of rough gray hair outlined his mouth, and his watery eyes were pinched half closed behind a pair of scummy glasses. He spit a wad of chewing tobacco way out in the street.

"He's been out looking for you'uns a long while now," Fuzzy said. He jerked his head toward the diner. "Your moms is both fit to be tied. You two best git on in there."

Tommy and I gave each other a worried look. Something inside my head warned me to run, to follow the railroad tracks out past the cornfields and the old Myron glass factory, on into the next county. Instead, I rested my bike against the side of the building and pushed the door open.

My jaw dropped as soon as we stepped inside. The diner was full of people, mostly Wishers. Some of Daddy's brothers were hunched over a table, smoking cigarettes and playing euchre. A bunch of my Wisher cousins were piled into a corner booth, and it looked like every single one of them had a giant root beer float.

"Jeez! What's going on? What're they doing here?" Tommy pointed to our sheriff, Bud Castor, and his deputy, Denny, who stood behind the counter with Mama and Aunt Charlene.

Tommy and I had always made fun of Bud and Denny, calling them Castor Oil and Deputy Chipmunk Cheeks behind their backs. Today, though, the sight of Denny's fat, rosy cheeks didn't make me want to laugh. And Castor Oil had a look on his face that made me want to slink back out the door.

"Hey! You guys!" yelled my little sister, Carla, waving wildly from her perch on top of Mama's counter. "Guess what? Guess what happened?" She pulled a sucker from her mouth, jumped off the counter, then raced over to us. "Our daddies just robbed a bank!"

Chapter 3

My hands flew to my mouth. I could hardly catch my breath; it felt like I'd been walloped in the chest with a baseball bat. Tommy's face turned bright pink.

"You're lying," I said to Carla. But deep down I knew it must be true. Why else would the sheriff be huddled behind the counter with Mama and Aunt Charlene? And what about Daddy's family? Why would they be there? Most of them avoided Mama like she had a bad case of the measles, except for Daddy's youngest brother, Uncle Russell. He owned a used car lot on the outskirts of Myron and liked to drum up business at her diner. Besides, I'd heard Mama say once that the only time the Wishers got together was to celebrate bad news.

"I ain't either lying!" Carla cried. She hurled her sucker at my face. I threw my Turkish taffy back at her. It clipped her in the eye, and she let out a wail.

"I'll bet you a thousand million dollars it's true! Our

daddies robbed a bank, and now they're 'scaped. They've gone and run off with the money," Carla said.

"Billie," Mama called from behind the counter. "You and Tommy get over here."

My head buzzed with questions. I sped around the tables, knocking into Uncle Russell. He reared back, brushing his elbow against a tall glass of Coca-Cola. It spilled all over his tight lime green pants. "Hell's bells!" he said, whisking the ice and soda off his lap. "Watch out, gal! These pants are brand-new."

"Sorry," I said, but I didn't stop to help him clean up the mess. I followed Tommy behind the counter.

"Where's Daddy?" I asked Mama straight out.

"What bank did they rob?" Tommy asked. "How come we didn't hear any sirens?"

"They hit the Henderson County Bank," Aunt Charlene said. "More money in Millerstown, I guess." She fumbled through her pocketbook and pulled out a pack of Chesterfield cigarettes. "Looks like they got away with a trunkful of it, too—more than I'll ever see in a lifetime." Her hands shook when she struck the match.

"Where's Daddy?" I said again, louder this time. I pictured

him in handcuffs, squashed in the back of a sheriff's car between two mean-looking guards. Hot tears welled up behind my eyes, and I fought the urge to cry.

"Oh, for God's sake, Billie. I don't know." Mama pulled me to her, giving me a tight hug. "It just happened a little while ago. Nobody knows where they went, honey. They got away." She brushed a tangle of curls off my forehead, then took a bobby pin from her apron pocket and pinned my hair back over my ear. "Bud thinks they may be on their way north."

"Your daddies ever talk to you about anybody they know up in Indianapolis?" Castor Oil asked us. He yanked his shoulders way back and puffed his chest out. I stared him in the eye and said no. Tommy stood silent beside me, chewing on his thumbnail.

"Well, if either one of them is to try and contact you, I want you to tell me or Denny right away. We're working with the Millerstown force on this." Bud rocked back on his heels and gave us a wink.

I nodded, but here's what I thought: It'll be a hot day at the North Pole before I ever tell you where my daddy's hid, Bud Castor Oil.

I knew something, though, as sure as I stood there: about where Daddy was. And it wasn't Indianapolis. The thought hit me out of the blue, causing dribbles of sweat to pop out on my forehead. I wanted to tell Tommy right then, but I didn't dare. I couldn't take a chance on anyone hearing me.

I played dumb, making sure I didn't let on to Castor Oil what I was thinking. Mama sliced me and Tommy each a piece of sugar cream pie, then shooed us over to a booth by our cousins while she went outside with Aunt Charlene and Bud.

The bottom of my thighs squeaked across the orange vinyl as I slid over the seat. Carla sat across from us, licking a fresh grape sucker Mama had given her. She snarled at me, but I ignored her. I was too busy listening to my uncles talk about the holdup.

"Heard they squealed out of Millerstown so fast nobody could've caught them," Uncle Russell said. He dumped a mountain of ketchup on his french fries.

"Must've burned all the dang rubber off them tires," another uncle said. "Bud heard they left skid marks all the way down Main Street."

Uncle Russell looked around, then leaned over the table and dropped his voice. I had to crane my head way back to hear him. "I'm bettin' they ain't far from here. We'll be hearing from them real soon about a new ve-hic-le, mark my words."

My heart pounded. Did Uncle Russell know what I suspected, that Daddy was hiding close by?

"I wonder whose car they were driving. My dad's car doesn't go near that fast," Tommy said.

"They was driving a *git-a-way* car," Carla said. "'Cause they had to git away from the policemen. That's what Bud Castor told Mama."

I sat stony-faced, not wanting to believe what I'd heard. I couldn't imagine my own daddy had robbed a bank. Somebody must've made a mistake. He wasn't a criminal! I knew he'd been in a little trouble with the law before he'd gone off to California, because I'd overheard Mama talking about it. When I'd asked her the details, all she'd said was: "He pulled a reckless stunt with Warren. Honestly. That man needs to grow up and think for himself, quit doing everything Warren tells him to do."

But that had been three years ago, so I was pretty sure

Daddy had done all his growing up by now. Maybe this whole bank robbery business was a case of mistaken identity—the kind of thing that happens in detective books.

"How do the cops know for sure Daddy and Uncle Warren are the robbers?" I asked Uncle Russell.

He leaned back, taking a drag off his cigarette. "Because the dumb asses didn't have nothing but bandannas tied over their mouths, that's why. They was easy to identify."

Carla burst out laughing; it always tickled her when a grown-up cussed. "Whitey Hudson knowed right away who they was. He was in the bank, and he told on them. That's what Mama said anyways."

Whitey Hudson? I almost threw up right there. Wouldn't you know that nosy old fart—Daddy Joe's uncle—would be an eyewitness and go blab it all? I pictured Whitey squinting his eyes behind those thick glasses, sticking his neck out a mile to get a good look at the bank robbers.

"Whitey doesn't know everything," I said. "I bet he made a mistake. Mirabelle says he's half blind, anyway. He probably just thought he saw Daddy and Uncle Warren."

My voice sounded high and whiny, like it belonged to someone else.

"Nope. No mistake," Uncle Russell said. "Whitey swore to it. Says he was there on church business when it happened. Scared the tar out of him."

"Hell, Whitey wasn't the only one to recognize them," someone else said. "One of the tellers knew who Warren was."

"Don't know what the heck those two were thinking," Uncle Russell muttered. "Dumbest thing I ever heard, robbing a bank where everyone knows you. They must've been desperate; probably something to do with that IOU Warren's racked up with them hoods in Indy."

So that was it. Uncle Warren owed money to some Indianapolis crooks. I should've figured the robbery had been his idea. I just couldn't understand why Daddy had gone along with him this time.

"What's going to happen if they get caught?" Tommy asked.

"I reckon they'll end up at Pendleton," Uncle Russell said.

No! Not Pendleton. That scared me enough to make my teeth chatter. They couldn't take Daddy to the Pendleton

Penitentiary. I'd known about that place ever since I was a little kid. It was just a few miles west of Myron, a long row of flat gray buildings surrounded by guard towers and barbed wire fence. I got cold chills every time we drove by there.

I'd heard only the worst criminals in Indiana got sent to Pendleton: guys like Vaughn Watson, who'd shot and killed his own brother in downtown Myron a few years ago. I'd never known him, but I knew his son, Goble, who was meaner than a snake. If Daddy got caught, he'd be in the same prison as Goble Watson's dad—maybe even the same cell.

That's when I decided I had to find Daddy quick, before the police captured him. If I could convince him to surrender and give the money back right away, maybe him and Uncle Warren wouldn't get sent to Pendleton. Maybe the judge would let them off with a couple of months in the county jail.

I wanted to talk to Tommy about it, but the diner had gotten so busy I couldn't ever catch him alone. I wandered through the afternoon in a haze of cigarette smoke, jukebox music, and Wishers joking around. The news about

Daddy and Uncle Warren didn't seem to bother any of them. In fact, they acted like it was downright funny, whooping and slapping each other on the back. I figured Mama was right: The only reason they'd shown up was to celebrate bad news and brag about all the crazy stuff any of them had ever done over the last twenty years.

The robbery had become big news in Myron, too, especially since Millerstown was only five miles up the road. At least half the town had stopped by to hear the details. Nothing that exciting had happened since Vaughn Watson shot his brother.

Mama made me wait on customers, and every table I passed people were talking about Uncle Warren and Daddy. Their voices would hush into a whisper whenever I walked by, but I could still hear them, loud and clear. They might as well have been shouting from the top of the Myron water tower.

"That oldest Wisher, Warren, he's always been a troublemaker . . ."

". . . surprised to hear Earl was involved. He's wild, but I'd never thought he'd do anything so radical as stick up a bank . . ."

It went on like that all afternoon, until I wished I could yell, "FIRE! Everybody run for your lives." Finally, when Mama wasn't looking, I ducked into an empty booth, pretending to clean it. Aunt Charlene and Bud Castor were sitting in the booth next to me, huddled close together, talking real low. I was hoping Bud would say something about the search for Daddy and Uncle Warren. Maybe he'd gotten more news from the Millerstown cops.

I kept my nose buried in a plate of leftover mashed potatoes, watching Bud from the corner of my eye. He scooted closer to Aunt Charlene, then struck a match and lit her cigarette. She blew a puff of smoke over her shoulder. "Thanks. My nerves are shot," she said.

"I can see why," Bud said. "This has got to be hard on your boy."

Aunt Charlene shrugged. "I don't know how he's taking it. Tommy's not close to his dad; never has been. That bum's not paid a lick of attention to his own son all these years."

"Now that's a downright shame," Bud said.

"I know Billie's hurting, though," Aunt Charlene went on. "She adores her daddy. Always has, from the moment

Wanda brought her home from the hospital. Followed Earl around like a puppy as soon as she could crawl. It like to killed her when he left."

"Is that right?" Bud said. "You know, I never was real clear why Earl went to California in the first place. All I heard was he got laid off from Firestone, then went to work with his brother on some good-paying construction job out West."

"You want to hear the *real* story?" Aunt Charlene said, her voice husky and secretive.

Bud tilted his head toward her. "Sure enough."

I slumped farther down in my booth so they couldn't see me. My heartbeat pounded in my ears.

"Earl didn't get laid off from Firestone," she said. "He got canned."

Chapter 4

Daddy got canned? What was Aunt Charlene talking about anyway?

I bit hard on my knuckles to keep from jumping up and telling her to get the facts straight. Daddy hadn't been fired from his job at Firestone. He'd explained it all to Mama; I'd heard him. "Work's slowing down at the factory," he'd said. "They had to lay off a couple of us new guys."

But I could tell Castor Oil was lapping up every word Aunt Charlene said. He scooted even closer to her. So close you couldn't have slid a hair between them.

"Yep," Aunt Charlene told Bud. "Something fishy was going on, so Joe let Earl go. Joe made it look like a layoff, though, to protect Wanda and the kids."

"Now that's news to me," Bud said. "Never heard it."

"That's because Joe never breathed a word of it until Wanda pressed him for the facts. You know, he's carried a torch for her since high school. But then he went off to Korea and Wanda took up with Earl."

"Now ain't that something?" Bud said. "He's a stand-up guy, that Joe Hughes."

My ears turned hot as ash. Joe Hughes isn't any stand-up guy, I wanted to shout. He's nothing but a fake. If Daddy had really been fired, then Mr. Joe Hughes had done it on purpose, just so he could get rid of Daddy and win Mama over for himself.

"Yep, Joe's a keeper, all right," Aunt Charlene said. She snapped her pocketbook open and pulled out a mirror, then patted her stiff yellow beehive into place. Aunt Charlene was a beautician at Miss Mona's Beauty Parlor in Myron, and she prided herself on wearing the most fashionable hairstyles.

I slipped away when Uncle Russell came over and started talking to Bud about the good deals at his used car lot, but I couldn't forget a word of what Aunt Charlene had said. It weighed on my mind like a sandbag all afternoon. Why had Mama married Joe Hughes when she knew he'd fired Daddy? Couldn't she see what he'd been up to? I didn't say anything about what I'd overheard, but as the day wore on, I got madder and madder at her and Daddy Joe. I avoided talking to her as much as possible, even when she tracked me down in the kitchen of the diner and tried to hug me, asking if I felt all right.

By late afternoon I guess I'd heard fifty different versions of the bank robbery, each one worse than the last. And I still hadn't told Tommy my hunch about Daddy and Uncle Warren's hideaway. I hadn't had a chance to get him by himself. He'd been ignoring me and hanging around my uncles and cousins, acting more and more puffed up as the day wore on.

"You think this is going to be on the radio?" Tommy asked Uncle Russell.

"Reckon so. It'll probably be on the television news, too. This here's pretty big-time stuff."

That made Tommy's head swell even more. I could hardly stand the way he swaggered around in front of our cousins, acting like we were related to Jesse James or something. By the time Ernestine came to the diner to see me, I couldn't wait to get away from everyone.

"Come on," I said. "Let's go outside."

We sat on the concrete bench outside Fuzzy's Tavern,

where I filled her in on everything that'd happened.

Ernestine handed me a piece of her Bazooka bubble gum. "Gee whiz! I'm sorry about your daddy. What's going to happen if he gets caught?"

I tore off the wrapper and stuffed the gum in my mouth. "He ain't going to get caught. He's out of state by now, probably up near Washington, D.C." I didn't plan on lying to Ernestine. It just came out that way. She'd never been too good with secrets, so I wasn't keen on letting her know my suspicions about Daddy's hideaway.

She gasped. "For real? You think they're going all the way to Washington, D.C.?"

"Yeah, I'm pretty sure of it. Or else they may be headed up to New York City." I picked up a rock from the sidewalk and scratched a tic-tac-toe game between us.

"What will they do there?"

"I don't know. Probably look for a place to live or something."

I made an X in the middle box and handed Ernestine the rock. She thought for a while before she scratched an O in a bottom corner. "If I robbed a bank," she said, "I'd share all the money with poor people. You know, like

Robin Hood or something. You think your daddy will do anything like that?"

I shrugged.

"Why do you think they did it?" Ernestine asked.

"It was because of Uncle Warren. He owes money to some crooks in Indianapolis." I scratched an X above Ernestine's O.

The diner door swung open, and Mama came outside with Charlene and Bud Castor. "I'm going to Millerstown, Billie," Mama said. "The detectives told Bud a couple of our things are in your dad and Warren's apartment. Charlene's going to take care of the diner while we're gone. I want you to watch Carla until Joe gets back."

"How come he's coming back here? I thought he was at work," I said.

"He's getting off early," Mama said, "to help out with Carla."

"I can watch Carla by myself. I don't need any help from him. All he wants to do is shove his nose in my business."

Mama grabbed my arm and steered me up the sidewalk, away from the others. She leaned so close to my face I could've counted her eyelashes.

"You listen to me, young lady, and listen good." She clenched her teeth together, the words pinging out of her mouth like sparks. "I don't need one . . . single . . . solitary word of back talk from your smart mouth right now. You understand?"

I glared at her, jerking my arm from her grasp. Without giving her the satisfaction of an answer, I stomped back inside.

Chapter 5

Daddy's family didn't clear out of the diner until after suppertime. They left the place a mess, too. Sticky pie dishes and root beer float mugs sat stacked on the counter, knives and forks were tossed everywhere, and I found ketchup smeared all over the booth where my cousins had been sitting. On top of that, someone had even used the ketchup to scribble a dirty word across the middle of the table, except they'd spelled it wrong.

When Daddy Joe came to get Carla, he took one look at the place and said, "Billie, I'd like for you and Tommy to take care of these dishes and clean the tables. Your mother could use the help."

I snatched a rag from under the counter and, behind his back, started flicking crumbs onto the floor. How come he always stuck me with the dirty work? If he wanted the place cleaned up so bad, why didn't he do it himself?

Daddy Joe found Carla curled up asleep in one of the

booths. When he went to pick her up, he noticed the grape sucker stuck to a clump of her hair. He tried to untangle it, but it wouldn't budge. I would've just yanked it right out. Daddy Joe didn't, though. He shook his head and chuckled. "Guess your mama will have to take care of that," he said, then flopped Carla over his shoulder like a sack of potatoes. She never even made a peep.

She's the lucky one, I thought, as Daddy Joe patted her on the back. She gets treated like a cute little princess for having candy stuck in her hair, while I have to clean the whole diner.

"Don't dawdle, Billie," Daddy Joe said, his voice sounding even gruffer than usual. "You kids need to get home soon. Your mom doesn't like you out after dark."

Once he left, I threw my wet dish towel at the closed door. "Bossy jackass. I wish he'd been the one who robbed a bank. I wish he was the one going to Pendleton."

"Yeah. Next time I'm going to tell him to mind his own business. How come he's always picking on us anyway? This ain't even our mess," Tommy said.

We started hauling dirty dishes back to the kitchen and stacking them in the sink. I didn't waste a minute before telling Tommy my news.

"I know where our dads are."

Tommy stood with his back against the sink, holding a stack of plates. "No way. Not even the cops know that."

"Remember last week when Daddy took me and Carla to Millers Park Pool?"

"Yeah, but what does that have to do with anything?"

"Just listen," I said. "On our way to the pool, we stopped at Jim Dandy's." That's where Uncle Warren worked, the Millerstown Jim Dandy service station. "Daddy got out of the car to talk to your dad while he was pumping our gas."

"What? What did they say?" Tommy's eyes lit up with curiosity.

I took a deep breath. I hadn't thought much about Daddy and Uncle Warren's conversation at the time, but now the memory of it made my heart race.

"Daddy was standing behind the car, but I heard him say, 'I cleared it with Hinshaw,' and then your dad said, 'You sure we can trust him?'"

Tommy hadn't moved an inch. He kept staring at me, hugging the plates to his chest.

I went on. "Daddy said, 'Oh, we can trust him, all right.

He owes me. Besides, we won't need it for more than a few days, tops.'" I shivered as I told this to Tommy. I thought Daddy had been talking about borrowing something, but now I knew different.

"Well?" Tommy said, still staring at me.

"Well, what?"

"I don't get it. What's that supposed to mean?"

"It means our dads are going to hide out in Old Man Hinshaw's fishing cabin for a few days," I said. "That's what."

"No way! You mean crazy Old Man Hinshaw? He won't let our dads on his property. He'll shoot anyone who tries to go near that cabin."

Tommy was right: Old Man Hinshaw was crazy. "He's got a mental disorder," Mama had said. "Acts agreeable one minute, like a lunatic the next." Everyone in Myron knew that, and no one—probably not even Goble Watson—had enough nerve to go near his property. But Tommy didn't know the whole story about Daddy and Old Man Hinshaw, like I did.

Chapter 6

"Old Man Hinshaw owes Daddy a favor," I told Tommy. And then I went on to explain it. A couple of months ago, when Daddy had first come back from California, I rode with him and Uncle Russell to Millerstown. We'd taken Vernal Pike, the gravel road that ran by Old Man Hinshaw's property, and Daddy had let me steer the car.

We'd been laughing about how I'd almost run us in the ditch when we saw an old man on the side of the road. He was standing by a truck with its hood open.

"That's Fred Hinshaw," Daddy said to Uncle Russell. He steered our car to the side of the road. "Let's see if the old coot needs any help."

Uncle Russell had laughed. "Hope that dang gun ain't loaded," he'd said. I'd been a little nervous myself, because I'd always heard how Old Man Hinshaw would shoot anything that crossed his path. He'd acted real happy to see

Daddy and Uncle Russell, though. They both knew a lot about repairing cars, so it only took a few minutes for them to fix the problem.

"What do I owe you?" Old Man Hinshaw had said, pulling a worn wallet from his overalls pocket.

"Won't take a dime," Daddy said, getting back in the car. "My pleasure."

"Now you listen here. Fred Hinshaw pays his debts," Old Man Hinshaw said. He stuck his head in Daddy's open window. "You fish?"

"Like a shark," Daddy answered. "Love them catfish."

"Tell you what. You ever need a good fishing hole and a place to stay, you let me know. I'll put you up in my cabin a couple of nights."

"I'll remember that," Daddy had said.

Daddy and Uncle Russell had laughed about it on the way home, saying they might take Old Man Hinshaw up on his offer the next time they played poker. "Where the heck is that cabin anyway?" Uncle Russell asked Daddy.

"Way back in the sticks. Sits at the end of the lane that runs past the railroad bridge," Daddy said. "That crazy old goat doesn't know it, but I was out there a couple of times when I was a kid."

Tommy dropped the plates into the sink, letting them clang against the metal. He shook his head. "I still don't get it," he said. "Why would our dads want to hide out in some old cabin? They're rich now. Why wouldn't they just take off?"

"Because Daddy promised me he'd never ever take off again, that's why. He probably wants to take me with him or something."

"You ain't going, are you?"

Run off with Daddy? To tell the truth, I hadn't thought that far ahead. A shiver of excitement tingled up my arms when I pictured it, though. My daddy was so much fun; I imagined us tooling across the windy desert out west, stopping alongside the road to sightsee and camp out. "Throw me the fishing gear, baby," he'd call from the banks of the Mississippi River. "One dollar to whoever catches the biggest one." Maybe we could even go to the Grand Canyon, or Yellowstone National Park, where Daddy said grizzly bears roamed wild. My mind raced faster than a getaway car as I gathered another load of dishes.

"Maybe I will go with him," I said. "I'm sick of Mama and her turd-ball husband anyway."

"Oh, man! You can't take off with your dad. You'd never get away with it. Your mom would have every cop in the United States out looking for you. She'd have your dad thrown in Pendleton for life."

I didn't like hearing it, but I knew he was right. I couldn't go with Daddy, even if he wanted me to. It would break Mama's heart, and I'd never get to see Ernestine or Tommy or Carla again. There was only one way out of this mess. Daddy and Uncle Warren had to turn themselves in. They had to give the money back to the bank, and they had to do it right away. But would they both agree to it? I figured Daddy would if I cried my eyes out and begged him. I wasn't so sure about Uncle Warren, especially since he was in trouble with those crooks in Indianapolis. I asked Tommy what he thought.

"I dunno." He shrugged, heading out of the kitchen. I shook the last of the lipstick-smeared cigarette butts into the garbage can and followed him.

"You've got to talk him into it," I said. "You've got to

help me find them before the police do. We need to go out first thing tomorrow and look for that cabin."

"*We?* How come I need to go?" A look of alarm flickered across his face.

"Because he's your dad. Maybe he'll listen to you."

"He doesn't care what I say," Tommy said.

It was true Uncle Warren had never cared much what Tommy wanted, but I didn't let that stop me from nagging my cousin. After all, it'd been his dad's fault they'd robbed the bank in the first place, so it seemed only fair for Tommy to go along with me.

"Don't you want to help me find them? Don't you want to save them from going to Pendleton?" I said.

Tommy paced circles around me. "I ain't so sure about this. I ain't so sure it's a good idea. Besides, how're we going to find that cabin without going over the railroad bridge?" Ever since Randy Cruzan had died after falling off the bridge last November, Tommy swore he'd never go near it.

It took ten minutes more of coaxing and whining before I got him to even consider crossing the reservoir. What finally clinched it was the lie.

"We'll probably get one of those Good Citizen's awards, like they give out all the time in Indianapolis. I read about it in the newspaper," I said.

"What's a Good Citizen's award?"

"That's when the boss of the bank thanks whoever's helped get the stolen money back. They give you at least fifty dollars or something." I scrubbed at some pie meringue stuck to a counter stool, avoiding his eyes.

"No kidding? Fifty dollars?"

"Yep."

"Jeez, Louise! That's a lot of money."

"Yeah, sometimes they even give you more. It depends on how much money gets returned."

"Okay," he said. "I'll go. But I ain't so sure my dad will go along with anything."

I finished cleaning the gunk off the stool, flicking a pesky twinge of guilt to the back of my mind. I tried not to think too much about the fib I'd told him, because I knew in the long run, finding our dads was the right thing to do.

After carrying the rest of the dishes back to the kitchen, I took a good look at the mess of dirty pots, pans, and plates in the sink. I tossed my dishrag to the side.

"I ain't going to wash any of them," I said. Instead, I filled the sink with sudsy water, figuring the smartest thing would be to let the dishes soak overnight so Mama could take care of them first thing in the morning.

Tommy turned off the kitchen light, and we started for the front door of the diner. The sound of a person whistling—quick and shrill, like they were calling some-one—followed by a scuffling noise, startled us. I stiff-ened, and Tommy backed into the kitchen. "Who's that?" he whispered from the doorway. "You don't think it's our dads, do you?"

Of course! That had to be it. Daddy used to whistle for us kids all the time. He must be looking for me. I raced around the tables to the front door, then slipped outside.

Chapter 7

"**You** see anyone?" Tommy stood in the doorway while I checked up and down Main Street.

"Nuh-uh." I peered down the alley, then walked past Fuzzy's Tavern to the corner. "They ain't here. I bet they're still hiding."

It was then I noticed Tommy's bike leaned up next to mine, outside Mama's diner. We checked it out: the chain had been fixed, the handlebars and front wheel tightened, and a new padded seat replaced the torn one.

"Neat," Tommy said, pushing on the rubbery seat. Just as he swung his leg over the bike, three figures came around the corner from the other side of Fuzzy's.

Every single hair on my neck frizzed out when I recognized the teenage boy in the lead. It was Goble Watson, the meanest kid in Myron. And right on his heels tromped the dumb bunny Etchison twins, Herald and Gerald.

Goble whistled again, even shriller than before. "Hey, look," he said over his shoulder to the twins. "It ain't Billie-the-Kid no more; it's Billie-the-Bank-Robber's Kid." All three of them cracked up laughing like he was the world's funniest joke teller. Goble strutted over to us, planting himself in front of Tommy's bike. The Etchison twins hurried to either side, so the three of them had Tommy penned in. Goble's lips twisted into a sneer.

"What you punks up to? You out here looking for your big, bad daddios?" He shoved Tommy's handlebars.

My breath came out in quick spurts. Had Goble heard me talking about Daddy? "Shut up, turd. It ain't none of your business," I said.

"You're the one that better shut up, Wisher, if you know what's good for you." Goble coughed up something from the back of his throat and spit it right at me. A warm glob landed on the sleeve of my blouse, oozing down my arm. I wiped it on my handlebars, wanting to jump off my bike and ram my fist down his throat.

"You'd better leave her alone," Tommy said, but his voice squeaked like Mickey Mouse's.

Goble kicked Tommy's tire, snickering. "Yeah, or what, tough guy? You gonna run out and find your daddies to take care of you? You don't even know where they are."

I pushed my bike toward the street, my legs shaking so hard I could hardly walk. "Come on, Tommy. Let's go."

"You ain't going nowhere on that bike," Goble said to Tommy. He snatched the handlebars. "It's mine now."

I threw my own bike down and stomped back to Goble, until I wasn't more than an inch away from his ugly face. "You'd better cut it out or I'm telling."

"Who you gonna tell?" Goble crossed his eyes and made a stupid face at me. "You gonna tell your big, brave old man? Ooh, I'm all scared."

My whole body shook with anger. It didn't matter to me anymore that the three of them could've pounded us into pea soup. "Shut up, creep," I said. "At least my daddy ain't no murderer."

It got so quiet you could've heard a mosquito sneeze. Goble looked at me with hate in his eyes. I thought for sure he was going to rear back and slam me in the stomach, but the door to Fuzzy's Tavern opened. He started backing away.

"You're gonna be sorry you ever said that, Wisher." He nodded his head toward my bike. "Get that one, too," he said to the twins.

"No way," one of them said. "I ain't riding no girl's bike."

The tavern door closed again, and Goble and the twins took off down Main Street, knocking Tommy's bicycle around like it was a can of garbage. Goble stopped under a streetlight and looked back at me.

"You squeal, and something even worse will happen to your sissy cousin," he yelled.

I crossed my arms and shivered in the warm evening air.

Tommy kicked the street curb. "Stupid jerks. I really hate them."

Tommy grumbled about Goble and his bike the whole way home. He made me promise not to tell anyone, though. "Goble may try to get even with us. Besides, I don't want everyone calling me a sissy," he said.

When we rounded the corner by my house, Mama waved to me. Her and Aunt Charlene were leaning against the police car, talking to Bud Castor.

Tommy grabbed my arm. "Don't tell them about you-know-what," he said, sounding panicky.

I nodded, but the sight of Castor Oil's car had already made me forget about Tommy's bike. All I could think of was finding Daddy before the cops did.

"Joe tells me you two stayed to clean the diner," Mama said. "That's real sweet of you."

Aunt Charlene gave Tommy a bear hug right in front of Bud Castor, like he was only six years old. She always babied him like that. "That's my boy," she said, tousling Tommy's hair. "He's such a good helper."

I could tell Tommy was embarrassed by the way he wriggled out of her arms. "Aw, that's okay," he said, looking at the ground. "I didn't really mind."

"Billie," Mama said, "something came in the mail for you today. Joe brought it home from the post office." She led me to the porch and handed me an envelope. It was addressed to Miss Billieanne Wisher, in Daddy's handwriting. My fingers trembled as I took it from her.

"Hey," I said, noticing the torn envelope flap. "It's already been opened. Did Daddy Joe look inside?"

"Of course he didn't. I opened it."

"But it's mine! Daddy sent it to me, not you," I said, my voice rising. "It's none of your business." I couldn't believe it.

In the whole time Daddy had been back from California, Mama hadn't cared about one thing he had to say. But now she cared so much she was tearing into my mail.

"Oh, yes, it is my business, young lady. The man just robbed a bank. I've got to know what he's sending you in the mail."

I wanted to tell her I didn't care what she thought, that it didn't matter one bit to me. But then I saw Tommy watching us from the front yard, and I remembered our plans. If I got too sassy with Mama, she'd never let me out of the house in the morning. I swallowed my anger, mumbling, "I'm sorry."

"I understand, honey; really I do," Mama said, stroking my cheek. "Try not to take this so hard. What your daddy did doesn't have anything to do with you."

As soon as she headed back to Bud's car, I leaned over the porch railing. "Hey," I whispered to Tommy. "You're still going with me in the morning, right?"

He nodded, but he didn't look any too happy about it.

Then, holding tight to my envelope, I hurried inside and headed straight for the bedroom. I had to pass by Daddy Joe first. He was all stretched out in my favorite chair again, reading some book that was thicker than our school dictionary. He glanced up at me with a half smile, but I whizzed right by him without saying a word. I tiptoed into the bedroom so I wouldn't wake Carla. She was asleep on her back with her mouth hanging open, and little snores gurgled from the back of her throat with each breath she took. The grape sucker was still stuck in her hair.

My hands shook so hard I could hardly pull the card out of the envelope. On the front of it was a sun rising over the horizon. "Happy Birthday, Sunshine!" the card said. "Your bright smile lights up my life." When I opened it, a five-dollar bill fell out. "Dear Billie," Daddy had written, "I'm sorry not to be there on your birthday. Here's some money to get yourself a nice present from Clarksons. You and Carla be good and mind your mama now. P.S. I haven't forgot about that bike! Love, Daddy."

Chapter 8

I sat on the edge of the bed, barely breathing, staring at the bill in my hands. I could hardly stop my teeth from chattering. Had this money come from the bank robbery?

No, it couldn't have, I told myself. Because the envelope was postmarked from Millerstown, June 18. That was yesterday, a day before the robbery.

Carla rustled behind me. I checked to make sure she wasn't awake before stuffing the bill in my top drawer, under my socks. I didn't want her to know about it; she'd start begging me right off to buy her that Kimmy doll she'd seen at Clarksons'.

It wasn't really the money I cared about, though. I'd much rather have had Daddy back than any five-dollar bill.

I lay on my bed next to Carla, staring up at the dark ceiling, wondering why Daddy had robbed that bank. Had he only gone along to help Uncle Warren? It's true Daddy was loyal to his brother; he'd always been that way. I remembered the argument he'd had with Mama and Daddy Joe about it a couple of weeks ago. I'd come in the diner through the kitchen door, and the three of them had been out front.

"I don't want the kids at your apartment when Warren's there," Mama had said.

"Hell's bells, Wanda," Daddy answered her. "He lives there. I'm not going to kick my brother out of his own home. He's stood by me through a lot; you ought to know that."

"He may be your brother," Mama said, "but he's trouble. Joe says he's hanging out with some rough people."

"Oh, so Joe knows it all now, does he?" Daddy said. "Knows all about my brother, too? Why don't you take what Joe says and stuff—"

"That's enough." Daddy Joe's gruff voice had chilled my insides. "I won't have you talking to Wanda like that."

That was the kind of thing Daddy Joe always did—butt into our business like that. And Mama? I couldn't figure her, either. She was the one who wouldn't let Daddy come home, so of course, he'd moved in with Uncle Warren. It made good sense to me; where else did she expect him to live?

But as I lay there, my mind kept going back to why Daddy had robbed the bank in the first place. Was it really to help Uncle Warren out of trouble, or had he just wanted the money? Once, when Mama was furious at him, I'd heard her say Daddy was worthless. She said he'd inherited bad blood from his grandpa, just like all the Wisher brothers. I wondered if that could be true. Did being worthless really run in the blood? If it did, I might be doomed, too, because I'd been told a million times I was the spitting image of Daddy.

And then my thoughts turned to when Daddy had first come back from California. If only Mama had given him a chance, none of this would've happened. We'd be a family again, instead of all torn apart. I knew he still loved her. I remembered the day he'd come back, the day Mama told him she was marrying Joe. I'd been helping Carla get ready for bed.

I'd heard the front door open, and then Mama yelled, "Oh my God!" like a robber had burst in on her.

Carla and I hurried to the kitchen to see what the matter was. Daddy had been standing at the door with flowers in his hand and a smile on his face. It was the same smile I'd missed for three whole years, the smile Mama said could charm the stripes off a tiger.

Carla hadn't recognized him. She'd stood riveted to the floor, staring at him like he was a stranger. But I'd run straight into his open arms. "How's my girl?" Daddy had said, his eyes tearing up. "You know how much I've missed you, baby?"

That's when Mama started in on him. "You have some nerve, Earl Wisher, to come barging through that door, scaring the daylights out of me, confusing these girls."

Daddy ignored her. He'd sat down and coaxed Carla over. She climbed on one of his knees; I sat on the other. For the next half hour, while Mama banged around the kitchen, slamming dishes everywhere, Daddy told us how much he'd missed us. He told us all about California, how he'd picked oranges off of trees and swam in the ocean.

"Did you see sharks, Daddy?" Carla had asked him, wide-eyed.

"Oh, baby, did I see sharks!" he said. "Big as our house, and their teeth looked like this. Grrrr!" He'd bared his teeth and started tickling her, making her scream with giggles. It was just like he'd never left.

The good times hadn't gone on for very long, though. Mama had finally shooed us girls to bed. Carla fell asleep, but I snuck back down the hallway. I stood outside the kitchen, listening to them.

"I want to move back," Daddy had said. "I want to start over, prove to you I can turn things around."

Mama wouldn't have it. "It's too late, Earl. I've moved on."

"What's that supposed to mean?"

"I'm marrying Joe Hughes. That's what it means," Mama said. "And you'd better not cause any problems about it."

I'd heard a noise, like Daddy was choking back a sob. "Come on, Wanda! Give me another chance, babe. I've changed. And what about the girls? They want me back."

"If you cared so much for your daughters, why didn't you send money? Why didn't you answer Billie's letters? It broke her heart not to hear from you."

"Money was tight. I couldn't help it, babe. I was on the move a lot."

But Mama hadn't wanted to listen. "You go on now,"

she'd said. "I'll let you see the girls, but I don't want you hanging around this house."

Carla flopped over in the bed, startling me out of my thoughts. I got up and headed to the kitchen for a drink, peeking in the living room on my way. Mama and Daddy Joe were wrapped around each other on the couch, like usual, watching a show on the new television set he'd just bought her.

"Mmm," Mama purred. "Thanks for the back rub. That was nice and relaxing."

"Anytime."

Ugh. There they went again with all the lovey-dovey stuff. I held in a gag and headed back to my room.

"Bud says the Millerstown police think Warren and Earl are definitely somewhere in the area."

This time Mama's voice locked my feet in place.

"He says the state police will find them in no time. They've got a statewide search out for the car they stole."

"What about Billie? Will she—"

A loud hoot of laughter from the television drowned him out. I inched closer to the doorway, stretching my neck as far as possible to hear what he was saying, but

Mama picked that very second to get up and turn off the television. "I've been worried about that, too," she said, heading my way. "We'll have to keep an eye on her."

I hurried back to bed, but I still couldn't sleep. Why did Mama think they'd have to keep an eye on me? What kind of idea had Daddy Joe planted in her head? Why couldn't he mind his own business for once?

I tossed and turned forever. I couldn't quit worrying about Daddy, wondering if the cops would find him before I did. One minute I'd be mad at him for what he'd done; the next minute I'd picture him locked in a cold, dark cell at Pendleton. I fell asleep a couple of times, then woke right back up, worried Tommy and I wouldn't be able to find Old Man Hinshaw's cabin in the morning. It must've been past midnight when the hall light came on. The next thing I knew Daddy Joe was standing in my doorway. His shadow stretched across the room like a long black ghost.

"Billie?"

I didn't answer.

"Billie," he said again, his deep voice making me shiver. "I heard you tossing around in here. Why don't you go lie down by your mama tonight? I'll sleep out on the sofa."

I stayed flat on my back, my eyes squeezed shut, waiting for him to leave. After what seemed like forever, he finally turned away and headed down the hall.

I jumped out of bed and watched as he disappeared into the kitchen, then grabbed my pillow and headed for Mama's room. I flicked off the hall light, closed her door, and climbed onto the big four-poster bed. I curled up next to Mama and listened to the soft sound of her breathing, wondering what tomorrow morning would bring.

Chapter 9

My plan had been to wake up early, get Tommy, then head out on the railroad tracks toward the woods. But wouldn't you know it, Whitey Hudson messed everything up.

Instead of looking for Daddy, by nine o'clock that morning I was on my hands and knees with Tommy and Ernestine, pulling weeds out of Mirabelle's vegetable garden.

Whitey had barely waited until the milkman showed up before he rung Mama on the telephone, tattling on the three of us.

Of course, she flew into a fit after hanging up the phone. "You kids smashed their flowers? How many times have I told you to keep out of other people's yards?" She looked at Daddy Joe like she wanted him to agree with her, but he didn't say anything. I thought I saw a grin flicker across his face; then he rustled his magazine and buried his head behind it, probably studying up on some news about taxes or politics. That's the kind of stuff he always liked to read about.

I yanked a handful of weeds and cursed our bad luck. I'd have rather spit-shined ashtrays than spent one more minute crawling around Whitey's feet, listening to him and his prissy show-off granddaughter, Ada Jane, carry on about what had happened yesterday.

"Yes sir, I'd call this a fair punishment," Whitey said as I tossed the weeds into an old bucket. "A good day of weeding won't hardly make up for all the time Mirabelle put into them gladiolas, though. You young'uns have got to learn to have respect for people's private property. The Lord teaches, 'You reap what you sow,' and that there's a good life lesson for you. For your daddies, too."

Whitey kept following us, grunting and wheezing and fanning himself in the hot sun. He pulled a stiff yellowed handkerchief from his pocket, coughed up some gunk in it, then used it to wipe the sweat off his forehead.

Ernestine made a gagging sound from the tomato row. When I looked over at her, she pointed to Whitey and stuck her finger down her throat. Tommy and I both snorted into our hands.

"You'd better git inside here, Whitey," Mirabelle yelled from the porch. "You're going to be laid out flat with that asthma if you don't watch yourself."

"In a minute," he answered, then turned back to us. "Yes sir, it near put me in my grave, them two daddies of yours waving guns around like they was gonna shoot the whole place up. Had to take today off work just to recover."

Ada Jane fluttered her eyelids and shivered. She glanced over her shoulder like someone was after her.

"I'm scared, Grandpa. Do you think the police will catch them? What if they come back and try to rob someone else?"

Whitey chuckled. "I reckon them two is on a fast boat to China, honey. They ain't going to be hanging around this area no more. Doubt it, anyways."

"I hope they're gone forever," Ada Jane said. "No offense, Billie." She looked down at me, her nose all puckered up like she'd just smelled a stinkbug.

I fought the urge to smear dirt on her fancy white tennis shoes. Ada Jane was my same age, and we'd spent a lot of time together when Mirabelle baby-sat me and Tommy— too much time if you ask me. We weren't what you'd call best friends. In fact, we could hardly stand each other. The worst fight we'd ever gotten into was when she'd called Tommy trailer trash. I'd had scratches on my face for a week from her fingernails, but she'd been the one to finally yell "uncle." There'd been at least eight kids watching us, and Ada Jane had never gotten over losing to me.

She sidled up next to Whitey, pointing the toe of her shoe at a squash plant. "You missed some here, Billie. Ernestine's bucket has way more weeds than yours and Tommy's. Doesn't it, Ernestine?"

That was the other thing about Ada Jane. She was always trying to steal Ernestine away from me. They lived next door to each other, and Ada Jane couldn't stand it that we were best friends. She'd done everything she could think of to turn Ernestine against me, even lying about me to Ernestine's mom.

Ernestine looked in her bucket and shrugged. "I don't know. I ain't been counting."

I coughed back a laugh, then pulled a muddy clump from the bucket and shook it on Ada Jane's sock. When she noticed what I was doing, she tried to step on my hand, but I scurried down the row of yellow squash.

We worked like that for another hour or so, with Ada Jane bossing me and Tommy around—and sharing her lemonade only with Ernestine—until Whitey said he felt sick.

"It's the asthma. I'm going to have to lie down," he told Mirabelle. "You kids can go on home now, but I want you back here on Saturday bright and early to finish this up. And then you'll need to help set up for the church picnic."

I nodded at Whitey with a serious face, like I'd be ready to tackle his chores on Saturday, but my heart had begun to race. In a couple of minutes Tommy and I could start looking for our dads.

"You want to come over to my house, Billie?" Ernestine asked.

"Uh, no. I can't," I fibbed. "Mama said I had to go straight home. I'll see you tomorrow, though."

"I'll come over, Ernestine," Ada Jane said, sidling up to her. "And I'll let you use my roller skates if you let me ride your new bike." She smirked at me, then looped her arm through Ernestine's.

Ernestine rolled her eyes, like skating with Ada Jane was the last thing she ever wanted to do. Even though I couldn't wait to take off after Daddy, I felt a twinge of jealousy when they left.

"Let's go," I said to Tommy once they'd crossed the street. "If we hurry, we can be back in a couple of hours. Our moms will never find out."

I tugged his arm at the same time Daddy Joe's station wagon pulled up in front of Whitey's house.

Shoot! Not again. Why was he always bothering me?

Chapter 10

Daddy Joe stuck his head out the car window. "You need to come home and watch your sister, Billie. You kids hop in and I'll give you a ride."

What? I thought *he* was supposed to watch Carla. Wasn't that the very thing he'd promised Mama this morning?

"We don't need a ride," I said. "We'll walk."

Daddy Joe got out of the car and opened the back door. "Get in," he said. "I got called in to work. I'll drop you off on my way."

I glared at the mole on the back of his neck the whole way home, grinding my teeth so hard it felt like I had lockjaw. Time was ticking away faster than Carla poured sugar, and there wasn't anything I could do about it. There was no way we'd make it out to Old Man Hinshaw's that afternoon.

Daddy Joe left right away for work, so I got stuck with Carla for six straight hours. Plus he'd left me a list of chores. "I'd like you to pitch in and help your mother," he said. "She'll appreciate it."

Well, Mr. Stand-up-guy Joe Hughes had told another whopper. Mama got home at five-thirty, too worn out to appreciate anything except her easy chair. She didn't even look at the furniture I'd dusted or the dishes I'd washed. And to top it off, she was too tired to cook. "I was swamped today," she said, heaving her legs up on the footstool. "Why don't you make us up some grilled cheese sandwiches, Billie? You're so good at that."

She didn't say anything about Daddy, and I didn't ask. I was too scared to talk about it, too scared I might give away my secret. I kept quiet all during dinner, thinking how Tommy and I could slip off tomorrow morning. I didn't even argue with Carla when she whined that I'd burnt her sandwich.

After dark I ran across the street to Tommy's trailer. Aunt Charlene was sitting outside, painting her fingernails. "Hey there, honey," she said. "You feeling any better about things today?"

"Yeah, I'm okay." I stuck my head inside the trailer door. "Where's Tommy?"

"He's in his bedroom, sorting stones. I swear that boy could lose track of his shadow whenever he's messing with those rocks."

Aunt Charlene was right. I had to sit on top of Tommy's arrowheads to get him to pay attention to me. "We'll go first thing in the morning," I said. "Don't oversleep."

"You sure you know how to find the cabin?" he asked me, looking doubtful.

"Of course I do. The lane runs right past the far end of the railroad bridge."

When I said "railroad bridge," Tommy flinched.

The next morning I got up with the songbirds. I was lacing my shoes when Mama poked her head in my bedroom door. "I'm glad you're awake," she said. "I'm going to Indianapolis to meet with a couple of my suppliers. Margaret called in with a stomach virus this morning, so she won't be able to open the diner. Charlene's going to help out before she goes to work, but Joe says it's too much for her to do alone. He says that you, him, and Carla can pitch in."

She might as well have stuck my finger in a light socket; that's how shocked I was. Daddy Joe said *I* could help at the diner? Since when was he in charge of everything, and why hadn't anyone bothered to ask me?

I guess I shouldn't have been surprised, even though it wasn't fair. It seemed like Mama's worker, Margaret, was sick with the stomach virus every other day. And Mama never asked me if I wanted to fill in for her; she just told me I had to. It was always "Billie, I need help scrambling eggs this morning" or "Billie, get those tables cleaned, please; they're a sight." That's the way it'd been ever since Daddy Joe bought the diner for her.

I finished getting dressed and hurried over to Tommy's. "You mean we can't go out looking for our dads this morning?" He frowned like he was all blue over the news. I could tell he was more relieved than disappointed, though, because he didn't look one bit happier when I told him we could go after lunch.

Aunt Charlene stood at the bathroom mirror, fluffing her hair and dabbing perfume behind her ears. "Tell your daddy Joe to get the first pot of coffee on," she said as I left. "I'll be down there in ten minutes."

Mama left me a list of instructions longer than our church bulletin, mostly "don't do this" and "don't do that." "I'll be there at noon," she wrote, "before Aunt Charlene leaves. I want you and Carla to mind Daddy Joe. Remember! Put a smile on your face for the customers."

She should've left that note for Daddy Joe; he's the one who didn't crack a grin. I smiled until my mouth was stiff, all morning long while I waited on customers, even though I couldn't think about anything except finding Daddy. Besides that, I cleaned tables and washed dishes and helped Aunt Charlene scramble eggs.

But here's what Daddy Joe did: nothing. Unless you want to count tinkering with the faucet and the pipes and the back door as work. When Aunt Charlene asked him what he wanted to do, wait tables or help in the kitchen, he said, "Oh, you and Billie can handle that. I'll take care of some maintenance problems."

Carla followed Daddy Joe around all morning, doing nothing with him. She had her bride doll in one hand and his tool belt in the other. He nodded at everything she said, pretending to be interested in her chatter about dolls and how much she wanted "the best doll of all—a Kimmy doll."

He didn't pay me one bit of attention, though, not even to say, "Those dishes look real clean, Billie."

It was different when my real daddy came to the diner, back when Mama was just a waitress there. Daddy liked to be out front with the customers. He knew everyone, and he'd goof around with people, laughing and joking and getting them to stay forever and order coffee and pie, just so they could hang out with him. I remembered the day Daddy told a tableful of Mama's lady friends, "Free banana cream pie on the house." He'd cut each of them a giant piece, then brought them all a free drink, too. They'd gushed over him like he was a movie star.

But Mama hadn't been all that happy about it. Like usual, she'd jumped all over Daddy when everyone left. "Now who's going to pay for the three pies?" she'd said. "Me? Because Roy"—he was the restaurant owner back then—"will have a cow when we come up short."

"Relax," Daddy had told her. "It's only pie. He'll never miss it. Besides, we're doing the man a favor. It's good public relations."

Mama had grumbled so much Daddy finally said, "Okay, okay. Don't say anything to Roy; just let me take care of it."

You sure wouldn't catch Daddy Joe giving out free pie.

He even reminded Aunt Charlene to charge for the second coffee refill. "It's the little things that add up to making money," he said.

The morning dragged by slower than Whitey Hudson's benediction prayers. Finally, ten minutes before noon, Mama showed up. I'd never been so happy to see her in my life, until she laid another bombshell on me.

"Billie," she said, "Joe's worn out. You'll need to stay home and watch Carla this afternoon while he sleeps. And make sure you keep the noise down."

He's tired? I thought. How come? I was the one who'd done all the work.

I paced around the house all afternoon, watching Carla play dolls, itching to get away. What if Tommy and I missed Daddy and Uncle Warren? I knew they couldn't stay at Old Man Hinshaw's cabin forever.

Two whole days had passed since the robbery, and I wasn't one bit closer to tracking Daddy down.

When I woke up Saturday, I was hoping everyone had forgotten about Whitey's garden and the church picnic. Mama might have, because she had a lot on her mind. But not Daddy Joe. Oh no. He never forgot anything that involved chores, and sticking his nose in my life seemed to be his favorite pastime. He looked at his watch when I walked in the kitchen. "You'd better get hopping. Whitey called; says there's some weeding left. He's expecting you and Tommy at nine."

"I don't see why we have to go back over there," I said. "It's not fair. We already pulled a bunch of weeds on Thursday, way more than a bucket full. If you ask me, Whitey's just too lazy to do it himself."

Daddy Joe spit coffee back into his cup, and his eyes widened like I'd just said a string of cusswords. I couldn't tell if he wanted to laugh or yell at me. All he said was: "Well, if I recall it correctly, I didn't ask you. It's your responsibility. And you'd better get going before your mother gets another phone call from Whitey."

But he's your uncle, not mine, I thought. Maybe you should tell him to quit phoning our house about every little thing.

Ada Jane was stretched out on a lawn chair, a happy smirk on her face. She sipped at her lemonade while Tommy,

Ernestine, and I got our gardening instructions from Whitey. "And once you kids are done out here," he said, "you can help Mirabelle set up for the church picnic." He hooked his thumbs around his tight belt. Two of his shirt buttons had popped open, and his hairy white belly looked ready to burst into the sunlight any second now. "That oughta take a good two hours or so."

My heart sunk. For the third day in a row it didn't look like we'd make it to the cabin.

"Whitey," Mirabelle called out the window, "Ralph Clarkson's here. He's got that collection money ready for the bank. Says it's a nice bundle."

"Send him on back," Whitey said. "I'm keeping my eye on these kids."

Mr. Clarkson followed Mirabelle out the back door. He'd barely set his foot in the yard before he started talking to Whitey about the bank robbery. "Guess you had the hellfire scared out of you on Wednesday, huh?"

"Ain't that the truth?" Mirabelle butted in. "Got his asthma goin' again. I was afeared he'd go into a full-blown attack."

"Now that's too bad," Mr. Clarkson said, shaking his

head. He glanced down at me and Tommy real quick, then leaned toward Whitey and started whispering something. Mirabelle and Ada Jane moved in closer to him.

My heart turned a cartwheel. Did he have news about Daddy? I wanted to jump up off the ground and yell at Mr. Clarkson to speak up. Just when I thought I'd die of curiosity, Mirabelle reared her head back in surprise.

"What?" she screeched. "What's that, Ralph? You say the police found the robbers' carcasses alongside the road?"

Chapter 11

Carcasses! I fell against Tommy, my heart pumping so fast and hard I thought it would explode. Daddy was dead! They'd already found his body.

"No. You got it wrong," Whitey told Mirabelle. He pulled a dirty snot rag out of his pocket and used it to wipe the trickle of sweat from around his mouth. "He didn't say anything about a carcass. Did you, Ralph?"

I held my breath, watching Mr. Clarkson like a hawk eyes its next meal, waiting for his answer. He fidgeted with his shirt collar, his face turning pinker than a raspberry. "Er . . . um . . . well, what I meant to say was that the police has found the *robbers' car* alongside the road near Indianapolis. The engine's dead."

"You mean our dads got away?" Tommy blurted out.

"For real?" Ernestine asked.

"That's correct," Mr. Clarkson answered.

My body went limp with relief. I slumped over,

letting the breath I'd been holding hiss out of my nose.

"Hmph!" Mirabelle said. "Didn't hear you right. Guess I need me one of them dad-burned hearing aids."

Ada Jane giggled, and the three grown-ups went on talking about our dads like Tommy and I weren't even there. I pretended like I couldn't care less what they said.

Ernestine crawled over next to us. She handed Tommy and me each a stick of gum. "Golly! I'm glad your dads got away. I hope they make it to New York City okay."

"Yeah. Me, too." I took a shaky breath, but I couldn't get what Mr. Clarkson said out of my mind: The police had found the stolen getaway car on the way to Indianapolis, which was north of Myron. Old Man Hinshaw's cabin was south of Myron, the opposite direction. So where were Daddy and Uncle Warren? What if I'd been wrong? Suppose they hadn't gone to the cabin at all?

I started yanking weeds like crazy, urging Tommy to hurry up. We had to get out of that garden.

After a bit Mr. Clarkson began talking about the money from some church collection he'd brought with him. "Exactly three hundred and fifty-two dollars in here—thought you'd want to get that in the bank first thing Monday morning," he told Whitey.

Whitey took the long white envelope Mr. Clarkson handed him. "Thank you kindly, sir. I'll take this over to the church office in a bit. We should have another bundle to add to it after the picnic."

"Can I take the money, Grandpa? Please." Ada Jane cocked her head to the side and scrunched her lips into a smart little pout. "I know exactly where it goes."

"I reckon so. But you be careful, little lady. This money is going to help replace that old church organ your grandma's been playing." He handed the envelope to her like it was a top secret message from the president of the United States.

Ada Jane clutched it with both hands and flounced over to where we were working. "Grandpa," she yelled, "can Ernestine come with me? Pretty please with sugar on it. I don't want to go all by myself."

Ada Jane's sly-looking grin made me grit my teeth. I knew what she was up to: just another way to get Ernestine to herself. I wished a bolt of lightning would flash out of the sky and knock her into outer space, all the way to Pluto.

"I reckon that'll be okay. Go ahead and take your little friend," Whitey said. "But that don't mean she'll get out of doing any work. The two of you can help set up picnic tables."

Ada Jane skipped toward the back door. "I'll be right back, Ernestine. I'm going inside to get you and me something special."

Ernestine turned to me and Tommy. She crossed her eyes toward her nose, flapped her elbows like chicken wings, and stuck her twisted tongue out at Ada Jane's back. We cracked up laughing.

The second the back door closed Ernestine jumped up. "Uh . . . Mr. Hudson, sir," she called across the yard. She flashed her most dazzling smile, the one she always reserved for grown-ups. "Can Billie and Tommy go to the church with us, please? We'll probably need lots of help lifting those heavy picnic tables."

"No. I don't believe that's necessary," Whitey said. "These two can stay right here, under my supervision. They'll be over to help you later."

Ernestine plopped back down beside me. "Crud! I'm going to be stuck with that whiny Ada Jane all day. And she'll get me in trouble if I'm not nice to her. She always does."

"Come on, Ernestine," Ada Jane yelled from the door. "Grandma wants us to take these cupcakes to the church."

"Wait a minute there, little lady," Whitey said from the side of the house, where he was standing with Mr. Clarkson. "I wanted another word with these young'uns. It won't hurt you none to listen to this, too, Ada Jane." He shuffled toward us, wheezing with each step he took.

Ada Jane skipped down the porch steps and over to the garden. She pulled Ernestine up off the ground, then handed her a chocolate cupcake. "I made them myself," she bragged.

"You got any more?" Tommy asked.

"Nope. We have to save the rest for the picnic," Ada Jane said. She took a bite of hers.

"You don't want one," I said to Tommy. "If she made them, you'd probably keel over dead after the first bite."

"I heard that, Billie. You'd better shut up, or I'll tell your daddy Joe. He doesn't like your sassy mouth anyway. Grandma said so. She said he's planning to be real strict and shape you up, now that he's your stepdad."

"Now, now, girls. Let's stop the fussin'," Whitey said as he joined us. He put his arm around Ada Jane and started lecturing us about getting along with one another.

I was digging my finger in the ground, ignoring him, when something buzzed by my ear. I jerked my head back, watching from the corner of my eye as a giant yellow jacket latched onto a marigold next to Ada Jane's leg.

And then something set me off. Maybe it was the way Ada Jane had her arm looped through Ernestine's, or the smug smile that had settled on her face. Or maybe it was just how she seemed so tickled about Daddy and Uncle Warren's troubles. In one quick second I swatted at the yellow jacket, hoping it would get mad enough to go after her leg. It buzzed back at me. I swatted again, harder this time, but I sent the bee straight toward Whitey. He lurched back when it zoomed up and around his eyes. He let out a gasp of air, causing a third button to pop off his checkered shirt. The yellow jacket must've sensed a delicious snack then, because it dove straight into Whitey Hudson's big, bare belly and dug its stinger in.

Whitey yelped and stumbled backward. He grabbed his

stomach with both hands, his sweaty face turning a deep red. He started coughing and wheezing so hard he couldn't get a breath.

"Grandma!" Ada Jane screamed at the top of her lungs. "Hurry up and come quick! Grandpa Whitey got stung. He's having a fit!"

Chapter 12

We all followed Mirabelle as she rushed Whitey inside and settled him on the couch. She propped his head up with pillows, pulled off his glasses, then loosened his belt and took off his shoes and socks. She dragged a giant fan across the floor, plugged it in, and aimed it straight at Whitey's face. It whirred like an airplane propeller, blowing tufts of thin gray hair straight up off his head. She sent Tommy and me into the kitchen to scrape frost out of the icebox, which she used to pack over the welt on Whitey's stomach. By now it had swollen way up and turned candy apple red.

Mr. Clarkson watched everything from the other side of the room. He shuffled from one foot to the other, coughing softly into his hand. "Is there anything I can do?" he asked Mirabelle. "Can I run out for some medicine?"

"No, thank you, Ralph. He ain't allergic to bees that I know of, and I've been through this asthma stuff plenty.

What he needs is rest. He got hisself too worked up over that bank incident. It's a wonder he ain't worse than he is." She covered Whitey with a sheet, then sent us kids over to the church to help set up for the picnic.

"You're in charge, Ada Jane," Mirabelle said as we headed out the front door. "Git that organ money put up in your grandpa's special place—you know where that is— then I want all you kids to help in the kitchen. And no nonsense!"

I took one last peek over my shoulder at Whitey. He looked whiter than the cold cream Mama smeared on her face every night. I couldn't help feeling bad, seeing him stretched out sick on the couch like that.

"Uh . . . I . . . hope you get your breath back real soon, Whitey," I said.

For once in his life he didn't answer me with a sermon. He just nodded his head a bit.

The first thing Ada Jane did after the door closed behind us was take Ernestine's arm and start dragging her toward the church. "Come on, Ernestine," she said in her stuck-up voice. "I want to show you something."

I didn't care anymore what Ada Jane did, though. My

mind had turned to Daddy and Uncle Warren again. I had to find out if they'd made it to the cabin. That's when I decided Tommy and I would slip away the first chance we got. I hoped Ernestine wouldn't be mad at me for leaving her alone with Ada Jane all day, but I didn't see any way around it.

"Stay here," Ada Jane snapped at Tommy and me once we were inside the sanctuary. "I have something important to do with Ernestine, so don't you two go anywhere till we get back, or else I'll tell my grandma." Normally I would've told her exactly where her and her grandma could both go, but I didn't want to stir up trouble. I just wanted her to get lost for a minute, so Tommy and I could get out of there. She took off across the room, calling for Ernestine to follow her.

"Umm . . . I'll wait here with Billie while you put the money away," Ernestine said. She scooted closer to me.

Ada Jane was already halfway down the aisle. She spun back around, her hands landing on her hips. "My grandma said you're supposed to help me. She's going to get real mad if you don't."

"Just go ahead with her," I whispered. "I don't want to

get in any more trouble with Mirabelle." My chest tightened with guilt. I felt like a heel for tricking my best friend, but it was too late now to explain everything to her. I'd tell her later, after we'd found Daddy.

"Okay, okay, I'm coming." Ernestine followed Ada Jane toward the other end of the sanctuary. The old wooden floor creaked under their footsteps. Rays of morning sunlight shone through the stained glass windows, making a halo of dusty light over their heads. The farther away they got, the faster my heart thumped. I grabbed Tommy's arm the second they disappeared through the back of the sanctuary.

"What the—where're you going?" he asked, following me as I sped out the front door of the church.

"Come on!" I sailed down the steps, jumping two and three at a time, my heart pounding by now. Without looking back, we raced up the block, around the corner, and straight out of town along the railroad tracks. We didn't stop to rest until we'd made it to the old abandoned glass factory about a half mile away.

Tommy collapsed on the ground behind me, panting. "You sure you want to go all the way out past the bridge?" His voice held the hint of a whine.

"Of course I do," I said. We couldn't give up now; we were halfway there. "What's the matter? You too chicken to cross it?"

He jumped to his feet, yelling in my face, "I ain't a chicken! How come you always think you're some big, brave hotshot, huh? Like you're the only one who's got any guts or anything." He kicked the rocks and sent them spinning across the ditch.

"Well, if you aren't scared, why don't you want to go?"

"Aw, I don't know. I was thinking there may be cops around the reservoir. Castor Oil told my mom the state police might search the whole county. If they see us, they're going to want to know what we're doing out here."

I eyed him suspiciously. "How come you didn't tell me that earlier? You just made it up, didn't you?"

"No! I swear it. Bud said so. I just didn't think much about it until now, that's all."

I started down the tracks without him, thinking over what he'd just said. Was Bud Castor right? Would the state police really search the whole county—even Old Man Hinshaw's property? "Go ahead and do whatever you want," I called over my shoulder. "But I'm going. And I'm keeping all of the Good Citizen's award money if Daddy comes back with me."

"Okay, okay, I'll come," he said, catching up to me. "Just don't call me a chicken anymore, or you'll be sorry."

"I know you ain't a chicken. I was just saying that." I pushed his arm playfully, relieved to see a bit of a smile slide across his face.

Still following the tracks, we walked out of the woods and into an open meadow. The sun burned down on us from a cloudless sky. I brushed a swarm of gnats away from my sticky face, wishing we'd thought to bring something to drink.

We headed around a big bend and up an incline, the railroad rocks crunching under our feet. The farther we walked, the more worried I got. I pictured hundreds of policemen surrounding the cabin, their guns pulled. I started walking faster, but Tommy lagged behind me. I wondered if he'd changed his mind about going again.

"Hurry up!" I said.

"I'm coming, I'm coming. I don't see why you're in such a big rush anyway." He poked along, flicking pebbles with a long, skinny stick.

"You're the one who said the cops may search the whole county. What if they decide to look out here first? What if Old Man Hinshaw tells on our dads? We need to warn them, before there's a fight or something. Someone could get hurt."

I sped up the long hill, determined to find Daddy before anything bad happened. I didn't think he could hurt anyone, but I wasn't so sure about Uncle Warren. He was different than Daddy. He had a quick temper. Mama said he was like a firecracker, just waiting to get lit.

I was staring at the ground, still lost in thought, when Tommy poked me and said, "There it is—up ahead."

I looked up, and it took my breath. The railroad bridge stretched all the way out over the Oolitic Reservoir. We'd been trudging up and around the bend in the tracks for what felt like an hour, and by now we were sky high with nothing but rocky slopes on either side of us. The water glistened like it was a million miles away.

"It's pretty darn long," Tommy said, shading his eyes as he studied the bridge. From the expression on his face, I thought for sure he was going to turn and bolt right back to town.

"I ain't so sure we should do this. What if a train comes while we're out in the middle of it?" he said.

"I thought you weren't scared."

"I *ain't* scared! Maybe I just—"

I didn't get to hear what Tommy meant to say, though, because the long, low whistle of a train stopped him from uttering another word. The tracks vibrated under my feet. I stiffened. The whistle blew again, louder this time. I could hear the train steamrolling up the curvy hill we'd just climbed.

"We'd better get off here." My voice quivered. I swung around, looking frantically for a safe place to dodge the train. But where? We couldn't go forward, because then we'd be stuck on the bridge. If we retraced our steps, we'd meet the train head-on. My heart sunk when I realized there wasn't anything on either side of us but the steep, rocky hills.

I stood motionless, my mind numb, the tracks buzzing under my feet, the whistle making me cover my ears. I looked behind us again. Here it came, barreling full speed around the bend, heading straight up and at us. I couldn't see anything but the mouth of the engine, bigger than a cannon, chugging and grinding like it wanted to flatten us dead. I screamed and hopped off the tracks onto a narrow strip of gravel, bracing myself to dive straight down the side of the hill, yelling at Tommy to follow me. But he didn't move. He just stood there in the train's path, his arms rigid at his sides, his mouth frozen into a terrified gasp.

Chapter 13

By now the train was so close I could smell the red-hot sparks under its wheels. I screamed louder at Tommy. He still didn't move. I lunged at him, grabbing his arm, pulling him with a strength I never knew I had. He tripped over the tracks, falling into me like a hundred-pound sack of flour. The two of us tumbled headfirst down the slope, clutching at loose rocks and clumps of dirt—anything we could get hold of—to stop the fall. We skidded halfway down the hill before sliding into a shrub, where we lay crumpled against its prickly branches, panting like dogs. The train rumbled away.

Tommy lay flat on his back, his face ghostlike, his chest heaving with every breath he took. "Man. Oh, man. Oh, man. Oh, man," he said between gasps. "I told you so. I told you a train would come."

I sat stiff as a board, my heart racing. A sickening, clammy feeling crept over me. We'd nearly been killed.

I looked at him accusingly. "How come you didn't move out of the way? I thought you said you weren't scared."

"I wasn't scared. The darn train just surprised me, that's all." He sat up, moaning and groaning and massaging his ankle. "Man. This hurts like heck. Look, it's all swelled up. It got twisted when we fell off the tracks." He flopped on his back again, covering his eyes with his hand. "Jeez. There ain't no way I'll be able to make it over that bridge now."

I checked his ankle, inspecting every inch of it. "This ain't swollen. It's hardly even red."

"It is too swollen. I can feel it. My arm hurts, too."

I still couldn't see a thing wrong with his ankle, but I knew there was no arguing with him now. He wasn't going to cross the bridge. "So what are you going to do? Go home?"

"No way. I'll stay on the lookout in case Castor Oil or the state cops come along." His chest swelled up when he said, "I ain't going to let anyone get past me, that's for darn sure."

A pang of doubt crossed my mind. Should I go over the

bridge by myself? Or had what just happened with the train been a sign from God? Suppose He was warning us to stay away from Old Man Hinshaw's cabin. I wondered if we should just give up and head home, but the thought of Daddy being locked away in Pendleton tugged hard at my heart. I couldn't go back now. I had to find him. I had to convince him to turn himself in.

"Okay," I said. "I'll go by myself."

Once we made it back up the hill, I stood for a while and stared at the bridge. The long line of tracks was held up by giant blocks of concrete. The bridge was wide, too, maybe even wide enough to dodge a train. I knew how to swim, so if worse came to worst, I could jump into the reservoir. I took a deep breath, gathered all my courage, and started across the tracks.

"Watch out!" Tommy yelled before I'd even made it over the water.

I spun around, thinking another train was headed for me.

"Careful! You'll get killed if you fall," he shouted.

"Will you shut up! You almost made me have a heart attack."

I kept going, trying not to look down at the water. I tried not to think about how there weren't any guardrails, or what would happen if I got dizzy, or how Randy Cruzan had been acting crazy and fallen off the bridge last fall. He was dead now. Instead, I stared straight ahead and started humming "Onward Christian Soldiers," hoping to get God on my good side, at least until I'd made it to the end of the bridge.

The humming worked. It loosened me up, making me feel carefree, giddy almost, like I was a tightrope walker with a crowd of people below, all of them watching me breathlessly.

I turned to wave at Tommy, to let him know I'd almost made it over, but I didn't see him anywhere. He must've wandered back down the tracks—probably off somewhere looking for rocks. So much for all that business about his swollen ankle.

And that's when I heard it.

Boom! A shotgun blast.

I ducked, swallowing a scream.

My head spun like an earthquake was rocking everything around me, but I knew I had to get off the bridge. I took off again in a panic, trying to jump the last few crossties two at a time. That turned out to be a mistake, though, because my foot slipped out from under me and I fell forward, landing facedown near the edge of the bridge. With my heart thundering in my chest, I lay there still as a stone, staring at the water below me.

Finally, after convincing myself the gunshot had come from way out in the woods and hadn't been aimed at me, I got up on my knees and crawled the rest of the way off the bridge.

I'd never been out this far before, but I knew two things for certain: A wooded lane led to the cabin on Old Man Hinshaw's property, and the lane wasn't far from the railroad bridge. I knew this because Daddy had pointed it out to Uncle Russell that day they'd helped Old Man Hinshaw with his car. "That's the lane that leads back to his cabin," he'd said. "It runs by the railroad bridge."

It'd only been March, but it seemed like years ago when I'd been on that car trip with Uncle Russell and Daddy. I wondered if Daddy had any idea back then of the trouble he'd be in now. I wondered if he knew Uncle Warren and him would be running from the law, maybe even hiding out in the cabin. If Daddy had any inkling of what was to happen, he sure hadn't let on to me or Uncle Russell that day.

I found the lane right away. It wasn't much of a road, just a rocky pathway that wound through the woods and over a couple of hills. I followed it all the way to where it ended next to a giant pile of rubble, and that's when I saw Old Man Hinshaw's cabin.

I ducked behind a tree, holding my breath as I stared at it. The cabin sat in a small clearing, surrounded by a rusted barbed wire fence. Half the front porch had rotted away, the back part of its patchy tar paper roof was caved in, and even from where I stood, the two tiny front windows looked grimier than Fuzzy's Tavern floor. A lopsided sign in the front yard said: WARNING! THIS IS HINSHAW PRIVAT PROPERTY. TRESPASSORS WILL BE SHOT!

Could Daddy and Uncle Warren really be hiding out in that old shack? I didn't see any sign of them. Maybe they hadn't come here after all. Maybe I'd been wrong. Or what if they'd been here and left already? Should I check inside the cabin? Old Man Hinshaw's sign sure didn't sound like any joke. Suppose he caught me?

The stillness surrounding the shack made my skin crawl. I thought about Tommy on the other side of the bridge, waiting for me. I wished he would've come along.

A noise—like something rustling in the bushes—sent me to my knees. I peered around the trunk again, eyeing the cabin. I didn't see anything. It must be my imagination, I decided. I stood back up. I had to keep looking. I had to find out if Daddy was inside. I didn't want to yell for him, though; I worried Old Man Hinshaw might hear me.

I inched my way toward the barbed wire fence. Oh no! The gate was locked. How would I get over it? Just last summer I'd torn my leg climbing barbed wire at Grandpa's farm and had ended up with stitches. I looked at the scar on my calf and got cold chills, remembering how much it had hurt.

I was shaking too hard; I'd never make it over. Instead, I pushed one of the middle wires down as far as it would go and slowly, carefully started squeezing through it, praying the wire wouldn't snap out of my sweaty hands and gash my other leg open. I had one foot on each side of the fence when I felt a tug on my blouse—it'd gotten caught on a barb. I couldn't free it because both my hands were holding the wire down. As I swung my other leg through and pulled away from the fence, I felt my blouse rip at the shoulder. *Shoot.* I'd have to remember to hide it from Mama, maybe stuff it in the garbage when I got home.

I picked my way through the overgrown weeds and headed toward the cabin's porch. The closer I got, the faster my pulse raced. If Daddy was there, how come he hadn't called to me? More than anything I wanted him to fling the door open, grab me in his arms, and say, "Billie! I've made a bad mistake. Warren and me are taking this money back right now and turning ourselves in to the law."

The only thing that greeted me, though, was an uneasy silence. I tapped on the door. No answer. I pushed, and to my surprise, it creaked open.

"Hello?" I whispered. I took a tiny step inside. "Daddy? Are you in here? Is anybody here?"

Light from the open door spilled into the cabin, casting my shadow across the room. I looked around. An inch of dust topped every piece of broken-down furniture in there. The hot, stale air nearly suffocated me; it felt like a hundred degrees. I sneezed, then jumped back when I saw a deer's head hanging crooked on the wall. It stared right through me with sad, lifeless eyes. I was just about to tear away and climb back through the fence when I noticed something else. Something that stopped me cold. Something that gave it all away.

I knew he'd been there, because I smelled it, the faint scent of Daddy's aftershave lotion. I couldn't leave now. What if he was huddled somewhere in the cabin, injured? Or even dead? I ventured farther inside and saw two cots pushed up against a wall in the corner, a pile of threadbare sheets tossed over them. A long white envelope on an end table caught my eye. Was it a note from Daddy? I picked it up, my hands trembling, and a wad of bills fell to the floor—more money than I'd ever seen in my life.

I couldn't quit staring at the bills. The money was from the bank robbery. It had to be. But why was it here? Had Daddy and Uncle Warren forgotten it, or had they left it on purpose? It doesn't make any difference, I thought, dropping to the floor. I have to take it. Otherwise, Old

Man Hinshaw may find it. He might turn it over to the cops and tip them off about Daddy.

I snatched all the loose bills, stuffing them and the envelope into my pocket.

I started for the front door before hesitating. Maybe I should check out the second room of the cabin. It couldn't hurt anything. I might find some information about where Daddy and Uncle Warren had gone.

I tiptoed back across the creaky floor. Halfway there I heard a loud thump, like someone had bumped hard against something. My stomach nearly came up my throat. Was someone outside the cabin? I stopped and waited, holding my breath. I didn't hear anything else, so I forced myself to keep going, one tiny step at a time. When I got to the open doorway, a rubbery black spider swung through the air and dropped onto my arm. I shrieked, flinging it away, then lunged into a dingy little kitchen.

I looked around for signs of Daddy, but all I saw were a sink piled with dirty dishes and rotten food, a grimy old stove in the corner, and a refrigerator with its door hanging loose from the hinges. I moved toward the sink, thinking I'd check out the cabinet over it. As I reached for the knob, the front door of the cabin slammed open like a cyclone had blown against it.

"Hey, you! Trespasser!" came a man's shout from the other room. "Git out from wherever you are, or I'll shoot your durn head off!"

Chapter 14

I cowered against the wall, searching wildly for some-where—anywhere—to escape. The back door? Just when I started to run for it, the clump, clump, clump of heavy footsteps came my way. My knees locked. I felt paralyzed, like my feet were buried in wet cement. It was too late to hide now; he was right outside the kitchen.

With my eyes squeezed shut, I flattened myself against the wall and prepared for the gun blast. Instead, all I heard was the hissing of someone's breath, not a heartbeat away from my face.

"What in tarnation!" Old Man Hinshaw yelled.

My eyes flew open. He was standing over me, so close I could see up his hairy nostrils. His stale whiskey breath nearly knocked me to the ground.

"It ain't nothing but a dag-blasted young'un. What you doin' on this here private property, girl?" He stepped back, glaring at me over the barrel of a long shotgun. The only answer that came out of my mouth was a squeak.

Old Man Hinshaw wiped a greasy mat of hair out of his face and lowered his gun. I stared, openmouthed, into his bloodshot eyes.

"Answer me, girl! Answer me quick, before I git fired up. I ain't takin' kindly to no trespassers out here."

"I ain't a trespasser! I swear it. I'm—I'm lost, that's all. I can't find my way back to the bridge."

Old Man Hinshaw's lips stretched into a sly grin, showing a mouthful of rotten teeth. "Lost, eh? Sure you're not lookin' for someone?"

I shook my head, praying he wouldn't recognize me from that day in March.

"Speak up, girl! I asked if you was lookin' for someone."

"No sir."

"I might take your word for it, girl." He wiped a shirt sleeve across his runny nose. Then he looked over his shoulder and started mumbling real low, like he was talking to himself. "Ain't got time to worry with young'uns now. Gotta find those double-crossin' varmints, gonna git what's owed me. Okay, girl," he said aloud to me, "You git on out of here, now, and don't you come back. You got that?"

"I won't come back," I said, my voice cracking, "I promise." I edged backward, my eyes fixed on his gun. I bumped against the door and grabbed the knob, working it open, then tore away from the cabin and across the yard, sailing over the barbed wire fence like a high jumper. I raced back through the woods, my pulse pounding in my ears. Once I made it to the reservoir, my legs turned to Jell-O. I dropped onto my hands and knees and crawled all the way back over the railroad bridge.

I found Tommy sitting alongside the tracks, sorting through a pile of rocks. "Run!" I yelled. "Old Man Hinshaw's got a shotgun!"

We shot down the tracks faster than rabbits, not stopping even once to rest, until we'd made it all the way to the glass factory. By now my hair was soaked with sweat, and my blouse clung to my sticky back.

"Slow down," Tommy finally said, gasping for breath. "My ankle hurts."

I checked to make sure we weren't being followed, then dropped to the ground. Tommy plopped down beside me. He started badgering me with questions right away.

"What happened? Did you see our dads? Did my dad

ask where I was? Did Old Man Hinshaw chase you?"

All I could do was sputter and fumble for words, nodding "yes" or "no" like a marionette. The picture of Old Man Hinshaw's dirty, sneering face—of his long shotgun aimed at me—kept popping up in my mind. I stuck my hand in my pocket, curling my fingers around the thick wad of bills, remembering his words: "Gotta find those double-crossin' varmints; gonna git what's owed me."

All of a sudden it came to me what Old Man Hinshaw had been talking about. The money. Suppose the money in my pocket was Daddy's payoff to him? And then I felt the blood drain right out of my face. If that was true, I hadn't helped Daddy one bit by taking it. I'd only gotten him into more trouble with crazy Old Man Hinshaw.

The bills burned my fingers like hot ashes. I couldn't wait another second to tell Tommy.

"You won't believe what—"

"Hey! Over here," someone shouted.

"Oh, man. It's Goble and the twins," Tommy whispered. "We'd better get out of here quick."

We scrambled into the ditch that ran alongside the tracks. "Make sure to keep your head down," I warned Tommy.

There'd be trouble, for sure, if Goble saw us. He'd probably beat up both of us, maybe even find the money on me.

We headed toward town again, but it was hard to stay hidden in the ditch. Luckily Tommy spotted a narrow, weedy path leading away from the tracks. "Look," he said. "That's the shortcut to the ball diamond. Let's take it."

Still running, we followed the trail all the way to the Myron Park baseball field. By now my legs ached so bad I could barely keep going. I ran my tongue around my dry, cracked lips. I was so thirsty I could've drunk a gallon of water straight from the toilet at Fuzzy's Tavern.

The pathway opened into a playground beside the ball diamond, right next to a drinking fountain. Tommy got first dibs on the fountain, and I paced back and forth, fingering the bills in my pocket while he lapped up a gallon of warm water. I could hardly wait to tell him about the money. I grabbed a bundle of it, getting ready to pull it out and flash it under his nose. But out of the blue here came my little sister, Carla, dragging one of her old dolls by its ponytail across the dusty ground. She had a half-eaten Fudgsicle in her other hand and was yelling at us to wait up.

"Ha, ha, ha! Ho, ho, ho! Lookee here at what I got," she sang when she caught up to us. She waved the Fudgsicle in our faces like it was a magic wand.

My mouth watered. I couldn't take my eyes off the smooth frozen chocolate. "Where'd you get that?"

Carla snatched it away when I reached for it. "Daddy Joe bought it for me, but you can't have one, 'cause you guys were bad and run off from the church." She pranced around us, twirling the Fudgsicle in her mouth while blobs of chocolate dribbled down her chin and onto her blouse. "Besides, Daddy Joe's fresh out of money. He told me so."

"Dang," Tommy said. "I wish we had some money."

My hand twitched in my pocket. I had money. Lots of it. And no one knew anything about it but me. I fingered the bills; they felt slick and cool. My cheeks tingled with the thought of how rich I was. What would it hurt if I bought a couple of Fudgsicles? Why should I care? I had enough money to buy us each ten Fudgsicles if I wanted to. In fact, I could've bought a Fudgsicle for everyone in Myron, Indiana—maybe even the whole state of Indiana. I inched up to the concession stand.

Wait a minute, though. The money wasn't mine. If I spent

it, then Daddy wouldn't be able to give it back to the bank.

"You want something, hon?" the lady behind the counter said. Tommy and Carla stood a few feet away from me, watching.

"I didn't know you had money," Tommy said. "Get me a Fudgsicle."

"I want a cherry Popsicle, Billie!" Carla yelled.

The smells from the concession stand tickled my nose, making me dizzy with hunger. I could already feel that creamy, cold chocolate in my mouth. Maybe I'd get us all a hot dog, too, with mustard and pickle relish. And a root beer, because I was still thirsty. It felt so strange having all that money, like I could do anything I wanted. I wondered if Daddy felt the same way. He must have, because he had tons more money than I did. I wondered, too, if he felt real sorry about stealing it.

The lady rapped her fingers on the counter.

"Um . . ." I fidgeted, shifting my weight from one foot to the other, my hand still squeezing the bundle of bills. For a moment nothing seemed real, not even the money. It felt like I was watching myself from the top row of the bleachers, not knowing what I planned to do next. I hemmed and hawed again, looking over my shoulder at Tommy and Carla. What would they think if they knew I was about to spend stolen money? Would they still want the treats? Carla probably would, because she was too young to understand. What about Tommy, though? What would he think? Or Ernestine?

Or Mama?

By now I had two people in line behind me.

"You made up your mind yet?" the lady said.

My heart fluttered. What if I just spent a little of it—maybe fifty cents? That shouldn't cause Daddy any problems. I opened my mouth to tell her everything I wanted, but I couldn't force a word out. I couldn't even say "Fudgsicle," even though I wanted one so bad I could taste it. I backed away, my breath shooting out in quick spurts.

"I'm not getting anything," I said. "I'm just looking."

All of a sudden the money felt like a nest of spiders in my pocket. I had to get rid of it, do something with it. But what? If I turned it in to Bud Castor, he'd want to know where I found it. I could take it back to Old Man Hinshaw's, but I didn't know if I could talk Tommy into going with me again. I knew one thing for sure, though: If I kept the money, then I'd be just like Daddy—a thief.

I walked back to where Carla and Tommy were standing.

"How come you didn't get us a Fudgsicle?" Tommy said. "I thought you had money."

Carla licked the last of the chocolate off her fingers and wiped her hands all over her shorts. "Yeah, how come, Billie? You was supposed to get me a cherry Popsicle."

"You don't need any cherry Popsicle now," I scolded her. "You just had a treat." I turned to Tommy and whispered, "Let's go. I've got to tell you something."

"Nuh-uh. You ain't going nowhere." Carla wagged the stub of her Fudgsicle at me and shook her head. "Daddy Joe's looking for you, 'cause Mama's real mad."

"He can look all he wants. I don't care."

Tommy and I hadn't gone five steps before Daddy Joe waved us down.

Chapter 15

"Aw, man. Ada Jane must've ratted on us for leaving the church," Tommy said. "I told you. I told you we shouldn't do it."

"Just don't say anything," I whispered. "Don't say where we've been."

Sweat rolled down my back as Daddy Joe caught up to us. He took his sweet time, too. Each step he took seemed like an eternity, like he was trying to torture me with worry about what he wanted.

"Your mom's been looking for you everywhere, Billie," he said. "Something to do with leaving the church before you were supposed to. She thought you might be out here at the ball diamond."

"The only reason we left was because Ada Jane wouldn't quit bossing us around," I said. "We're going back, though. Right now. Aren't we, Tommy?"

"Uh, yeah. We're going right back," he said, avoiding Daddy Joe's eyes.

I dug the toe of my shoe in the sand, hoping Daddy Joe would say okay and leave us be. He cleared his throat. The silence between us grew wider than a glacier.

When I finally looked up at him, I couldn't tell what was running through his mind. Maybe he was just curious about Tommy's ripped T-shirt and my torn blouse and all of our scratches and bruises, but it seemed like the flicker of a grin played around his lips. He looked away and coughed, then turned back to me, real serious.

"Your mom's at the diner. She wants to see you. You two run on home now and wash up before you go over there. Better put some ointment over those scratches, too. Some of them look pretty deep."

"Okay," I said.

"You want to tell me what happened? Why you're all scratched up?"

I shrugged, acting like it was nothing. "Just messing around."

"Yeah," Tommy chimed in nervously. "We've been out . . . uh . . ."

I turned my head slightly, cutting him a look from the corner of my eye, mouthing, "Keep quiet."

". . . goofing off and looking for arrowheads and stuff." Tommy stuffed his hands in his pockets.

Daddy Joe eyed us awhile longer, making me fidget even more. He kind of grunted to himself, then took Carla's hand and walked away. Her sticky fingers got swallowed up in his while she danced along next to him, trying to keep up with his long strides.

As I watched them leave, a wave of sadness carried me back to a sunny summer day, way before my real daddy had left for California. I still remembered it perfectly. Daddy had been teaching me to ride my bike without training wheels. Once I'd finally gotten the hang of it, I'd taken off like a cannonball down our bumpy sidewalk. "Go, Billie, go!" Daddy had yelled, laughing and whooping at the top of his lungs. I'd got going so fast, though, that I couldn't brake, and I'd ended up crashing into a tree, scraping all the skin off my elbow. Daddy had rushed to me, scooped me up in his arms, and carried me all the way home. He'd pulled some ointment from the medicine cabinet and smeared it over my elbow, praising me the whole time.

"This kid's a tough one," he'd said to Mama. "Look at her battle scar. She's a Wisher, all right."

I looked down at the scratches on my legs, wondering if Daddy still cared about me as much as he did when I'd skinned my elbow. For the last few months—ever since he'd moved back—he'd been telling me how much he loved me, but as I fingered the stolen money in my pocket, I couldn't help thinking he had a funny way of showing it.

"Shoot!" Tommy kicked the ground. "If my mom finds out where we've been, I won't ever be able to leave home again. I'll be grounded for the next hundred years."

We left the ball field and headed up Church Street. The minute I was sure no one could see or hear us, I said, "I've got something to show you. But you've got to swear to God you'll never tell a soul."

"What?"

"Promise me you'll never tell first."

"Okay. I promise already," he said. "What is it?"

I pulled a wad of the money from my pocket. "I found this at the cabin. It's from the bank robbery."

"Oh, man!" His eyes bulged out of their sockets. "Jeez, Louise! That's got to be at least a couple of hundred bucks."

I'd never seen him so excited. He kept after me to stop and count it, so we ducked into Mrs. Sumner's yard—only three houses away from our church—and hid behind a giant peony bush, thinking we'd be out of sight. I dropped to the ground and dumped all of the bills out between us. Tommy snatched them up and started stacking them in piles, just like he always did with his rocks.

"What's that?" He nodded at a scrap of notebook paper lying on the ground. I picked it up. My stomach did a somersault when I recognized the handwriting.

"'Hinshaw,'" I read, "'Here's the $300 we agreed on. Had to get away. Laying low now. We're having a car delivered to your place in two or three weeks when the heat's died down. Remember, that was part of the deal, so keep it quiet. We don't want trouble.'"

"Wow," Tommy said. "What's going to happen now? This money must be Old Man Hinshaw's. If he thinks our dads cheated him, he'll kill them the minute they show up."

My hunch had been right. Sure enough, this was the payoff money, and I'd swiped it right out from under Old Man Hinshaw's nose. Now he thought Daddy and Uncle

Warren had double-crossed him. I didn't doubt for a minute he'd shoot them both. Wasn't that his motto? "Shoot first. Questions later."

"Pick up the money!" I snapped. "Hurry! We've got to take it back right away."

"What? Go back to Old Man Hinshaw's? You're nuts. No way I'm going back there—he'll kill us, too."

Just when I started telling Tommy to forget it, that I'd go by myself, I saw something coming our way that made every hair on my head sizzle.

"Hide it," I said. "Hurry! All of it."

"Why?"

All I could do was nod toward Mrs. Sumner's front porch. There came Mirabelle, clomping down the front steps with a pie in her hands. We could see her through the bush.

"You're in charge, Ada Jane," she said. "You girls git this pie over to the church kitchen right now. And don't drop it. Rhubarb is your grandpa's favorite." Her old-lady shoes scraped across the concrete on the other side of the peony bush.

Tommy and I snatched a handful of bills and dodged

under the bush, hiding the best we could. The note and most of the money still lay scattered on the grass.

"Is Grandpa Whitey going to be all right?" Ada Jane's goody-two-shoes voice made me want to gag.

"His nerves is shot, honey," Mirabelle said. "It ain't no wonder, all he's been through in the last two days. And them two kids running off with the money for my organ near killed him. I'd better get back to the church and check on him."

Sweat started pooling around my eyes. What was she talking about, "them two kids" running off with the money for her organ? Did she mean Tommy and me?

"Come on, Ernestine," Ada Jane said. "Let's take this pie and then go get our bikes. I'll let you ride mine if you let me ride yours."

"I need to check Billie's house first," Ernestine said. "I want to see if her and Tommy came back."

"Humph!" Mirabelle snorted. "If them two are anywhere around, they'd better be praying to God I don't get my hands on them."

I thought they'd turned to leave. I grabbed Daddy's note and dropped it under the bush beside my leg, then reached out to pick up the loose bills.

Tommy thumped me in the side. A short, squat shadow fell over my hand.

I froze.

A shiny black shoe missed my finger by an inch.

My heart stopped cold. What if Mirabelle saw the note? I snatched it with my left hand—still blocked from her view by the bush—and tried to stuff it in my pocket. I wasn't quick enough, though. Because at the same time, Mirabelle reached down and yanked me to my feet. The note missed my pocket and fell to the ground. It lay hidden under the bush.

Ada Jane clutched her throat and gasped, staring at all the money like it had just fallen from heaven. I couldn't tell if she was going to scream her head off or dance around in joyful circles.

My eyes locked with Ernestine's. A gum bubble hung out of her mouth. She looked down at the money, then back up at me. I could tell she was mad, from the way she scrunched her eyes at me. "Gee whiz, Billie," she finally said, stuffing the gum back in her mouth. "You were supposed to wait for me in the church. Where'd you guys go? And where'd you find all that money anyway?"

"Grandma, look!" Ada Jane squealed. "That's the same envelope Grandpa Whitey gave me. You were right. It was Billie and Tommy that took the deposit."

"Well! If that don't beat all." In one swift move, Mirabelle reached down and snatched the bills off the ground. "Hoodlums. Just like your fathers, and that's a fact. You ought to be ashamed of yourselves. You wait until Joe Hughes hears about this. He's going to pack both of you off to reform school."

Chapter 16

"We've got the culprits, Bud," Whitey said, his voice quivering with excitement into the telephone. Tommy and I stood next to the door of the preacher's office, quiet as midnight, trembling, waiting, watching Whitey spray spit all over the telephone receiver. He hadn't wasted a minute making his call after Mirabelle dragged us back to the church. "Yes sir," he boasted to Castor Oil, "Mirabelle and my granddaughter caught them red-handed."

"Don't say anything," I whispered when Whitey turned his back. "We can't give the hideout away. Besides, you swore you wouldn't."

Tommy's mouth tightened. I wasn't sure how long he could hold out, especially since he'd already reminded me at least ten times how none of this was his fault.

I heard a commotion in the hall and peeked through the slightly opened door. A group of ladies from Mirabelle's church club was headed our way.

"Isn't it a shame about those Wisher kids?" a tall, thin lady in the lead said. It was Mrs. Mitchell, one of Mirabelle's friends. "Mirabelle's been saying all morning she suspected those two."

I nudged Tommy away from the door where we couldn't be seen. Whitey stayed huddled over the telephone, droning on and on to Bud about our capture. He didn't seem to notice the conversation in the hall.

"Mirabelle's baby-sat them kids for years," another lady said. "She says they have a wild streak, just like their dads. Especially that little Billie."

"I saw that child at Wanda's yesterday. My goodness. She's a beauty—the spitting image of Earl," Mrs. Mitchell said.

A tongue clucked. "Now there's a rascal for you, and oh, boy, does he ever love the ladies. Followed my niece around like a tomcat not two days after his and Wanda's wedding."

"It's the gambling that was his downfall," Mrs. Mitchell said. "I heard that's what led up to the bank robbery."

Gossipy old hens. I knew what Daddy had done was wrong, but it wasn't any of their business. I bit my lip to keep from yelling at them to shut up.

"Warren's the mean one," Mrs. Mitchell said, dropping her voice. "Did you know he . . ." Their footsteps trailed down the hall.

I looked at Tommy. I knew he'd heard them, too, because he'd been poking me the whole time they were talking. As soon as his dad's name got brought up, he swung around and studied a portrait of the preacher's wife that was hanging on the wall.

Whitey finished his telephone business and escorted us outside, where we waited on the steps for Sheriff Castor Oil. By now the whole church was swarming with people setting up for the picnic. My cheeks burned with shame when Bud pulled up and whisked us into his car like we were bandits, right in front of everyone.

I couldn't stand to even look at Ernestine. The expression on her face made me cover my eyes. Did she think, like the others, that we were thieves? I sunk into the backseat of the police car, wishing everyone would quit staring at me, wishing I could fade into the upholstery.

"We didn't steal any money," I insisted when Bud questioned us later. He sat with Mama and Daddy Joe and Aunt Charlene around our kitchen table. Carla was squashed between Mama and Daddy Joe, her eyes big and round and confused. She was sucking her thumb, too. She hadn't sucked her thumb in over six months. I couldn't help thinking it was my fault she'd started up again.

Mama's face was set in a grim frown. Daddy Joe looked more curious than mad, but I noticed he watched Tommy and me real close. Aunt Charlene sniffled into a lacy pink handkerchief.

Whitey stood behind Bud, shaking his finger at me. "Now that there ain't the truth, little missy. Mirabelle caught you two; the money was laid out between you." He shoved his face in Bud's ear. "They must've been divvying it up."

"I already told you," I said. "We found that envelope on the ground by Mrs. Sumner's sidewalk. All we wanted to do was count it. Ain't that right, Tommy?" He nodded, his face pale and drawn.

I told myself we weren't really lying, just rearranging the facts a little. Besides, I didn't dare tell the whole story. That would send Castor Oil and Chipmunk Cheeks straight out to Old Man Hinshaw's cabin.

"So let me get this straight," Mama said, her words

clipped and angry. "You two ran off from the church, then—"

"Yes, ma'am. That they did," Whitey blurted out. "Ran off right after they—"

"Then somehow, after two hours passed by," Mama went on, ignoring Whitey, "you just *happened* into Mrs. Sumner's yard, where you just *happened* to find the envelope of money? Where were you all morning, after you left the church? That's what I'd like to know."

Aunt Charlene blew her nose long and loud. "I'd like to know, too. Where were you, Tommy?"

"It's just like we told you," he muttered. "We were messing around, looking for arrowheads." But Tommy looked scared, like he was ready to crack. I chewed at my lip, wishing he was tougher-skinned. He had a soft heart when it came to Aunt Charlene. What if he caved in and gave our secret away?

"I know where they was," Carla piped up. "They was at the ball diamond, wasn't they, Daddy Joe?"

Daddy Joe coughed. "Right," he said.

"'Cause Billie almost bought me and Tommy something," Carla went on. "But then she didn't."

"At the ball diamond spending money, huh?" Whitey said. "Now don't that beat the band. Guess I hadn't heard that story."

"I've already told Wanda about seeing the kids there," Daddy Joe said. His curt voice made it sound like that was the end of that.

The questioning went on and on, though, until I wanted to grab Tommy and run back out to Old Man Hinshaw's cabin. I'd rather face him again than look in Mama's doubtful eyes one more time.

Another bad thing was that Whitey swore the envelope contained $352, but all they found on me and Tommy—plus the money Mirabelle had grabbed from the ground—only added up to $300. We even had to empty our pockets in front of everyone to prove we didn't have more money hidden on us.

I thought about Daddy's note when I turned my pockets inside out, relieved that I'd dropped it under the bush. But what if the note blew down the street and someone found it? Somehow, I'd have to get back to Mrs. Sumner's house again and look for it.

"See there?" Whitey said when our pockets were

emptied. "Fifty-two dollars is gone, clear and simple." He turned to Bud. "That money was put in the church office by my granddaughter and her little friend. No one else but these young'uns here knowed nothing about it."

Somehow, Tommy and I got through all the quizzing and questions. We stuck to our story the whole afternoon, but I worried he couldn't keep the secret much longer.

"It ain't fair," he said later that night. We were talking through the window screen in his bedroom because I'd snuck over after Mama and Daddy Joe went to bed. "Now I'm in a bunch of trouble, and I ain't even the one who went to the cabin."

"You can't say anything now," I said. "That would mess everything up."

"Are you in bed yet, Tommy?" Aunt Charlene called from the other side of his door.

"Please don't tell," I begged him. "Not yet. We've got to find them first. We've got to give them a chance to turn themselves in. Daddy will come back and tell the truth. He'll tell them where the money's from—I know he will. Swear to me again! Swear you won't tell until I find him."

"Aw, heck. I swear it," he said. "I ain't no rat fink. I

just hope your dad shows up real soon, that's all."

Neither of us mentioned a word about his dad helping us out.

I spent practically the whole next day—my eleventh birthday—alone in Carla's and my room. No cake. No party. Nothing. I just sat on the bed for a hundred hours, listening to a thunderstorm brew in the distance and sewing the rip in my blouse that had sent Mama into a fit when she saw it.

Around noon, I heard a commotion in the kitchen; then Carla yelled that Mirabelle and Whitey were there. I peeked out the bedroom door. *Shoot!* What did they want?

Mama came out of the bathroom with her mop bucket, grumbling under her breath, and headed to the kitchen to join them. I followed, slipping silently down the hall.

"Hey, there! Glad you stopped by." Mama's sweet singsong voice—the phony one she used for big tippers at the diner—floated out from the kitchen. "Why don't you two sit here a minute with Joe while I change? I need to get out of these dirty work clothes."

I dove into the hall closet, burying myself in a bundle of heavy winter coats until her footsteps clipped by. The second her bedroom door closed, I cracked the closet door open, hoping to hear what they were talking about.

But the coats muffled the conversation. The only thing I could hear was Mirabelle's screechy voice say, "School for delinquents . . ."

I stuck my head all the way out the door, in time to hear Daddy Joe answer her. "Don't mention that to Wanda."

"What're you doing, Billie?" Carla yelled when she saw me. "How come you're in the closet?"

Later that night I hid outside Mama's bedroom, eavesdropping again. I had to, because I had to know if she knew something I didn't about Daddy.

"I'm at my wit's end with her," Mama said, sounding close to tears. "I don't know what to think about this. It's obvious she's acting up because of what Earl did. Charlene thinks the kids are looking for attention."

"I don't know. Something about this doesn't add up," Daddy Joe said. "If they had the church money, then where's the missing fifty-two dollars?"

"And that's another thing." Mama went on like she

didn't even hear him. "Whitey wants that money back. He's hell-bent on it."

"Don't worry about Whitey," Daddy Joe said. "I'll take care of him."

I heard a muffled sound, like Mama crying against his shoulder. I slipped back to my room and shooed Carla off my side of the bed. I listened to the thunder and the wind whip through the branches outside my window, more determined than ever to find Daddy.

Chapter 17

The next morning Aunt Charlene stopped by on her way to work at Miss Mona's Beauty Parlor. I overheard Mama telling her how Daddy Joe planned on giving the church fifty-two dollars to make up for the missing money. "He's pulling it out of the savings account this morning," she bragged. "That's the kind of guy he is."

"I wish I had one just like him," Aunt Charlene said.

I wish you did, too, I thought. In fact, I'll give you Mr. Joe Hughes himself.

Mirabelle called a few minutes later, and Mama set up a schedule for Tommy and me to work at the church with her for the next couple of weeks. That was part of our punishment.

"You're due there at ten," Mama said after hanging up the telephone. "I hear anything about you giving Mirabelle a hard time, there'll be hell to pay. You got that?" She stared at me with the same frown she'd been wearing last night.

"Yes, ma'am," I said.

Mama raised her eyebrows; I guess she wasn't used to not getting an argument from me. I didn't dare say anything, though, because I didn't want her starting in on what'd happened yesterday.

"May I be excused?" I said, carrying my breakfast dish to the sink.

"Billie, is there anything you'd like to tell me?"

"No," I said, because there wasn't the first thing Mama could do to help me, even if I spilled my guts. The way it was looking now, I'd never find Daddy before the cops did. I'd never have a chance to talk him into anything.

A long sigh escaped her mouth. "We'll talk about this later," she said, then left for the diner. Daddy Joe took Carla to the ball diamond to look for Popsicle sticks under the bleachers—she liked to glue them together and make things—and I headed for the church.

Mirabelle had a bucket of vinegar water ready for Tommy and me. She made us wash windows, my least favorite job in the world. The way my day was going so far, I might as well have been in the Pendleton Penitentiary myself.

Tommy wasn't his talkative self, either. Usually he would've tried to tell me the best way to wash windows, like he was an expert at it, but this morning he just did whatever I said. I worried he'd changed his mind about keeping our secret, but I didn't get a chance to ask him until Mirabelle went after rinse water.

"I ain't going to tell," he said. "I already swore it. I just don't want to stay home all summer, that's all. And I heard my mom telling Castor Oil last night that when I wasn't working here, I'd have to go to Miss Mona's with her. Man, I hate that place."

"Castor Oil came over?" The hairs on my arms tingled. "Did he say anything about our dads?"

"Naw, he just said a bunch of stupid stuff to my mom, about how he liked her perfume and her new hair color, that's all."

I was supposed to work at the diner that afternoon, but Mama had instructed me to go home for lunch first. Daddy Joe started right in on me when I got there, too. I hadn't been home but a minute when he told me to quit swigging out of the milk carton.

"It's impolite," he said.

Well of course it was impolite. Who didn't know that? But some people, like my real daddy, for example, didn't make a big stink over it. Daddy let us drink from the milk carton all the time. In fact, he swigged out of it himself when Mama wasn't looking.

"You set the table," Daddy Joe told me. And then he made lunch, if you want to call it that. He smeared half a cup of tuna fish salad between two pieces of rye bread and set it on my plate, alongside carrot sticks and peas.

I muffled a groan. Why couldn't he ever make good lunches, like my real daddy did? Daddy never made us eat stuff like peas and carrots. Most of the time me and him had fried bologna and potato chips, and Carla ate straight from the peanut butter jar with her finger.

Daddy didn't even care if we filled up on Twinkies, like that one Saturday he'd been playing cards with his brothers, right before he left for California.

"Carla won't eat the bologna," I'd yelled at Daddy from the kitchen. He was sitting at a card table in the living room with my uncles, deep into a game of poker.

"Give her the peanut butter jar," he answered.

"We're out of it," I said. By then Carla was bawling

about being so hungry her tummy hurt. I stood at the living room door, not knowing what to do.

"Shoot! Be right back," Daddy told his brothers. He'd raced all around the kitchen, throwing every cabinet door open until he found some Twinkie packages. "How does this look, kitten?" he'd asked Carla.

The only problem was that Mama waltzed in the door right as Carla finished her fourth Twinkie. I was only on my second, but after Mama saw all the wrappers and the cream smeared on Carla's face, she had a conniption fit. I didn't get what the big deal was. Daddy had given us Twinkies plenty of times for lunch, and we'd never gotten sick over them, but Mama marched straight into the living room and interrupted his poker game.

"What're you thinking, Earl Wisher?" she'd yelled. "I leave you in charge of lunch twice a week, and you can't even see to it these kids get a decent meal."

Daddy tried some fast talking to get out of that one. It didn't work, though, not that time, especially when Mama noticed the mess my uncles had made—cigar butts and empty Coca-Cola bottles everywhere. And then Daddy got mad at her, too, because my uncles had left before he'd had a chance to win his money back.

But today, with good old Joe Hughes running our lunchtime, there wasn't a Twinkie in sight. Carla pouted and pushed her plate away. "I don't want tuna fish, Daddy Joe," she said. "It gives me a bad stomachache. Billie don't like it, either. She said so. She said you're always making us eat stinking tuna fish, and she's stinking tired of it. Didn't you say that, Billie?"

I took a bite of my sandwich, not daring to look up.

"Is that right, Billie?" Daddy Joe asked. "You're stinking tired of tuna?"

"Go ahead, tell him, Billie," Carla said. She took a swig of her milk. "Can I have peanut butter instead of tuna fish, Daddy Joe?"

"Guess I can arrange that," he said. "But you'll still need to eat those peas and carrots. What about you, Billie?"

"Tuna's fine," I muttered, even though I wished I could spit it down the sink. I kept quiet and stared at my plate through the rest of lunch, while Carla about chattered my head off. I was going to have to talk to that girl, teach her the things she should never blab to grown-ups.

"Come on," I said to her after we'd cleared the table.

"Mama wants you to walk with me to the diner. She's going to have Aunt Charlene cut your hair."

We followed the alleys all the way downtown. I didn't want to run into anyone, so I told Carla we couldn't go on the sidewalks. "We're playing spies," I said. "We have to sneak all the way to Main Street."

The only person I felt like talking to was Ernestine, but her mom had answered their telephone when I'd tried calling early that morning. I'd hung up without saying anything.

We made it downtown without anyone seeing us. I thought we were safe. And everything would've been fine—I could've run across Main Street straight to Mama's diner—if it weren't for the penny Carla had begged off Daddy Joe.

Chapter 18

Carla and I were two doors down from Clarksons'. "I'm going to get a bubble gum," she said, pulling the penny from her pocket.

"Not now," I said. I'd just seen two of Ada Jane's Sunday school friends—Lou Ann Riggs and Rhonda Jackson—walk out of Clarksons' with hula hoops. They stopped in the middle of the sidewalk and started spinning the hoops around their waists. I was sure they'd heard about the stolen church money by now; they'd probably even been at the church when Tommy and I got taken away in Bud Castor's car.

"Daddy Joe said we had to go straight to the diner," I told Carla.

She stomped her foot. "That ain't so! He said I could buy a bubble gum."

"Hush up," I said, taking her hand.

She pulled away from me and headed straight toward

Clarksons'. "Daddy Joe said I could," she yelled over her shoulder. "I'm gonna tell him if you don't let me."

Lou Ann giggled and put her hand over her mouth, whispering something to Rhonda. My body tensed with dread. I had to face them; I didn't have a choice. If I didn't let Carla spend her penny, I'd be in even bigger trouble with Mama. I gritted my teeth and followed her, wishing I could yank those pigtails right off her head.

I sped around Lou Ann and Rhonda and headed for the open store door, but Carla stopped in her tracks. She cupped her hands around her eyes and stood quiet as her shadow, staring at the two-foot-tall Kimmy doll in the window. It was like that doll had placed a spell on her.

"I'm gonna get Daddy Joe to buy me one of them," she said, her voice breathless with excitement. "I betcha anything he will, don't you think so, Billie?"

Lou Ann spun her hula hoop around her waist and giggled again. "Why don't you get Billie to buy it? She's the one with all the money."

Carla shook her head. "Nuh-uh. Billie don't have no money."

"Oh, yes, she does," Rhonda said. "Her and Tommy stole it from the church."

"You're a big fat liar," Carla yelled. "Billie didn't steal. She said so."

"You'd better quit calling me a liar. It's your family that tells lies."

"And robs banks, too," Lou Ann said.

A tear trickled down Carla's cheek. She stuck her thumb in her mouth, and my blood began to boil. I pushed on Lou Ann's hula hoop. "Leave my sister alone."

I took Carla's hand and headed inside the door, right in time to hear Mrs. Clarkson mutter to her husband, "Watch that candy counter, Ralph. It's those Wisher kids."

When we got to the diner, the first thing I did was run in the kitchen and call Ernestine. I hung up for the second time that day when her mother answered.

Later I was scrubbing the floor around the kitchen sink when Mama interrupted me. "I want you to take Carla for her haircut," she said, poking her head in the kitchen. "It's too busy for me to get away."

"Can't she go by herself? I've got this whole dirty floor to take care of."

Mama narrowed her eyes at me. "Now that's a new one. I've never known you to enjoy scrubbing the kitchen."

I shrugged, turning my attention to a sticky spot by my knee.

"Why don't you tell me the real reason you don't want to go?" she said.

The goo wouldn't come up. I sprinkled scouring powder on my sponge and went at it again, hoping Mama would go back to her customers and forget about the haircut. I dreaded the thought of going into the beauty parlor, of everyone staring at me.

Mama stepped into the kitchen and leaned against the counter. "Okay, Billie, what's going on? Joe and I aren't swallowing your story about the money. We think there's something you're not telling us."

"Who cares what he thinks?"

I shouldn't have said it; I knew that the second it came out of my mouth. Mama shot across the kitchen and whisked me and my sponge right up off the floor. "I'll tell you what I care about, young lady. I care about the truth.

And I care about you showing respect. I want to know what really happened Saturday, and I aim to find out."

"I already told you the truth. We didn't steal any money. Tommy and I found the envelope under Mrs. Sumner's tree. Someone else must've dropped it there."

She didn't believe me, I could tell, but I was saved by Fuzzy Hilton, one of Mama's lunch regulars. "You got some hungry folks out here," he called from the diner.

"I'll talk to you later," Mama said to me through tight lips. "Right now, you take Carla for her haircut."

On the way to Miss Mona's I found out why Ernestine hadn't answered her phone: It's because she was riding bikes with Ada Jane. They whizzed right by Carla and me like we weren't even there, then threw their bikes down and disappeared into Clarksons'. I hurried Carla down another alley so we wouldn't have to see them come back out. I'd rather have had another measles vaccination than watch Ada Jane steal my best friend.

That night, after Mama had grilled me about the money and I'd stuck to my story for the hundredth time, I was straightening Carla's and my room. I checked my drawer for the five-dollar bill Daddy had sent me. I stared at it for a while, thinking how it'd been five days since the bank robbery. Five whole days, and nobody knew where they were. Not even the cops.

Carla was lining her dolls up on her side of the bed. She had at least ten of them, but she still hadn't stopped talking about the Kimmy doll. "Daddy Joe said no, he won't buy it yet," she complained. "He said I have to be real good and do all my chores for one month, and then he'll think about it."

She started brushing her Jenny doll's hair with Mama's best brush, but I didn't tell her not to. I pushed my five-dollar bill to the back of the drawer, where she wouldn't find it, then dusted the top of our dresser.

"Do you think our real daddy would buy me that Kimmy doll?" Carla asked. Her eyes were wide and curious.

"Sure he would, but he ain't here, so there's no use thinking about it."

"Where is he?" Carla's voice turned so soft I could barely hear her. "Mama said he ain't caught yet, but she says he will be soon. Do you think he'll get caught, Billie?"

"I don't know," I answered, almost choking on the

words. "But whatever happens, he'll be fine. Don't you worry, okay?"

After clearing Carla's dolls off the bed, I helped her into pajamas and tucked her in for the night. I snuggled up next to her as she hummed herself to sleep. I couldn't quit thinking about everything that'd happened, how all our summer plans with Daddy were ruined. If things had gone right, we'd be out doing everything he'd promised, fun stuff, like fishing and swimming and going to the county fair. "We'll have a blast this summer—just you, me, and Carla," Daddy had said only a month ago.

But things hadn't gone right. Daddy had messed everything up by robbing that bank, and now I didn't even know if he was still alive.

Chapter 19

Three more days dragged by, each of them oozing into the next so slow I thought I'd die of boredom. It was Friday, and I still hadn't talked to Ernestine. I hadn't seen her around town, either. I'd called her house a bunch of times, but no one ever answered the telephone.

Tommy had started acting mad at me, like it was my fault he couldn't leave his trailer except to go to the church or Miss Mona's Beauty Parlor. He must've complained a hundred times about how he'd be stuck at home until school started back up in August.

"We're never going to find our dads," he said while we dusted church pews that morning. "I think we should go ahead and tell the truth about the money." He kept his voice low, because Mirabelle was just a few feet away from us, polishing her organ.

"No one will believe us if we change our story now," I

said, trying to stay calm, to reason with him. "They'll think we're making it up."

"But you've got that note your dad wrote for proof, don't you? You said you went back to Mrs. Sumner's and got it."

I moved down the aisle, flicking my duster faster than a cat's tail. I was scared to tell him the truth. I'd gone back to get the note, all right, but the paper had been all wet and blurry, and I couldn't read a word it said. It must've gotten drenched by the thunderstorm that hit on my birthday.

He followed me, whispering over my shoulder, "Don't you? Don't you have the note? You said you found it."

I spotted a dust ball under the pew and darted after it.

"You'd better tell me right now if you have that note," Tommy said. His voice squeaked again, like he was starting to panic.

"Shh!" I jerked my head toward Mirabelle and whispered, "You know who might hear."

All of a sudden a loud, sour blast from Mirabelle's organ filled the sanctuary. She started pounding out her favorite hymn, "A Mighty Fortress Is Our God," and you couldn't have heard a train whistle over the music. Now I didn't have any excuse not to answer Tommy.

"Just tell me. You'd better tell me you got that note," he said.

"Okay, okay. I got it," I said. "I went back and found it, but it must've got wet or something. The ink's all smeared. You can't read it."

"Oh, man. We're done for. We're dead. We'll never be able to prove we didn't swipe that money now."

"Why don't you just shut up? We don't need that note anyway. We know what it said; Daddy told Old Man Hinshaw they'd be back at the cabin in a couple of weeks. That means we only have a week left."

"The note said a lot more than that," Tommy said. "It proves it was the bank money we had, not the church money. No one will ever believe us without it. Man! I can't believe you let it get drenched. Jeez."

"What do you mean, *I* let it get drenched?" My voice rose louder as Mirabelle's music blared around us. "How come you didn't get the stupid note yourself if you were so worried about it?"

"Because I ain't allowed out of the house, that's why."

"Well, I ain't allowed out, either. So it's not all my fault. At least my daddy will come back and tell the truth once we find them. He'll tell everyone it wasn't us who stole that money. And that's more than I can say for your pukey dad." I shook my duster over his face and stomped out of the sanctuary.

I headed straight to the diner without telling Mirabelle where I was going, so it wasn't five minutes before Mama got the call that I'd run out. I was already boiling eggs for egg salad when the phone rang. Mama beat me to it. "Uh-huh. Yes. She's here, Mirabelle." Mama tapped her foot and held the receiver a good ten inches from her ear, and I could hear Mirabelle ranting all the way over by the stove. "Yes. I understand. I'll talk to her. Thank you," Mama said. Her voice sounded clipped and impatient, like she had a salesman hounding her.

I fiddled with the flame on the stove, trying to get it just right so the water wouldn't boil over.

"What's that about?" Mama said. "Mirabelle tells me you left early."

"I didn't feel so good." Now the flame was too low, so I turned it back up.

"So you're sick? You need to go home to bed?"

"No. I'm feeling better now. Besides, I was all done dusting anyway." I still didn't have the heart to look at her. I was afraid I might break down and rush into her arms and tell her everything. I couldn't do that, though. I had to hold out until Daddy got back to Old Man Hinshaw's cabin. According to his note, that wouldn't be for another week.

But then it occurred to me that if I wasn't nice to Mama, I wouldn't have a chance of getting out of the house to look for him again. "I started some egg salad," I told her. "Daddy Joe said he likes the way I make it. Maybe we can take some home to him." I threw that in on purpose, figuring it would make her happy if I said something respectful about him for once.

"Are you trying to change the subject?" Mama said, looking at me suspiciously.

A tap on the back door saved me.

"Hey, Wanda," Mama's deliveryman said. "Got a big load out here. You got room for all of this?"

"I'll be right there, Hank."

"You watch the diner," she told me. "Let me know if anyone comes in."

So far Fuzzy was our only customer. He was sitting at the counter, drinking coffee, like he'd done every afternoon since I could remember. He grunted at me when I walked by; then, out of the blue, he said, "For what it's worth, not everyone thinks you kids took that money. Told your mom as much."

I muttered, "Thank you," and sat at a table near the window, resting my chin in my hands. I was thinking about Daddy when someone tapped on the window.

Ernestine!

I waved her in, but she shook her head no and waved me out.

"Go ahead outside and talk to your friend," Fuzzy said. "I ain't gonna need nothin'."

I raced out the door, practically tripping over my own feet. I couldn't wait to talk to Ernestine. She didn't look that thrilled to see me, though.

I sat next to her on the bench. "Where've you been? I've tried to call your house, but no one ever answers."

"We've been to my grandma's," she said. "We left on Tuesday and didn't get back until this morning."

"Bet you had fun, huh? Did your grandma lose her

choppers?" I joked, hoping that would crack her up. Ernestine hated visiting her grandparents, because her grandma always took her false teeth out during meals.

"Ha, ha, ha. Very funny," she said, but she didn't sound like she meant it.

"What's wrong? Are you mad at me?"

"How come you and Tommy left the church that day? You said you'd wait for me. You promised."

"You don't think we stole the money, do you?"

Ernestine pulled two pieces of bubble gum from her pocket and handed me one. I popped it in my mouth, secretly smiling, because now I knew she couldn't be all that mad.

"No, but everyone else does. Even my mom." Ernestine fidgeted with a button on her blouse. "She doesn't want me to hang out with you anymore. She says you're a bad influence. She wants me to be best friends with that stupid Ada Jane."

The blood drained from my heart in one huge whoosh. A sharp ache took its place. I couldn't imagine my life without Ernestine. Who would roller-skate with me? Who would stay up all night with me, giggling over the naked people in Daddy Joe's *National Geographics*? From the time we'd been in kindergarten, Ernestine, Tommy, and I had always done everything together. Mama even called us her fearsome threesome.

Ernestine scratched at the bench with a pebble. A warm summer breeze blew wisps of hair across my face, tickling my nose. Every so often the wind would pick up a leaf, causing it to dance around our feet and skip down the sidewalk.

"Are you going to?" I whispered, breaking the silence. I could hardly get the words out of my mouth.

"Going to what?"

"You know, be best friends with Ada Jane?"

"Not if you tell me the truth about where you and Tommy went that day, about where you really found that money."

My mind spun a quick web around my secret, wanting to hold it close, to protect Daddy. But I'd already hurt Ernestine's feelings by running off from the church without her. If I didn't tell her about the money, I'd hurt her even more. What if she never talked to me again?

"Cross your heart, hope to die you won't tell," I said.

"I swear on the Bible."

"We found the money in Old Man Hinshaw's cabin. It's from the bank robbery."

Ernestine's gum fell out of her mouth and landed on the sidewalk.

Chapter 20

"**I've** got something to tell you. Something that has to do with *the secret*," Ernestine whispered in the telephone that night. She called me right after supper.

"What?" I clutched the receiver to my ear, my heart pounding like a drum. I'd explained everything to her earlier—about Tommy almost getting hit by the train, about finding the money and the note and all about Old Man Hinshaw and his shotgun. She'd sworn over and over she wouldn't breathe a word of it, but I couldn't help worry that something had leaked out.

There was a scuffling noise in the background; then I heard Ernestine's mom calling her.

"Okay, Ada Jane," Ernestine sang to me in a high, fake voice. "I can't talk anymore now. I'll see you tomorrow, right after lunch. At. Our. Spot. I'll tell you all about it then. Byeee."

I knew what she meant by "our spot." It was the bench

outside Fuzzy's. But I couldn't figure what she wanted to tell me.

The next day I could hardly wait to report for work at Mama's diner. Like usual, Tommy and I cleaned the church with Mirabelle all morning. Mama had said we could both eat lunch at the diner, and I rushed him through our chores so we could leave by noon. On the way over I filled him in on everything I'd told Ernestine and how she had something important to tell us.

Mama had our lunch waiting at the corner booth: hamburger, pickles, and french fries, my favorite. It felt like I was in heaven, especially after eating Daddy Joe's lunches for the last week. I thought about Carla at home with him, wondering what he'd fixed for her today. Probably chicken pot pie. At least it wouldn't be tuna fish salad. Daddy Joe had promised Carla he'd never make it again.

I was clearing our table when Ernestine tapped on the window. "Hey!" I yelled, waving her in. The diner had just cleared out. Mama was in the kitchen, making meat loaves.

Ernestine stuck her head in the door, then put her finger over her mouth and jerked her head back. "I couldn't get away without her," she whispered.

"Aw, shoot!" Tommy said. "Look who's coming—Ada Jane the lamebrain."

Sure enough, Miss Prissy strutted up the sidewalk and in the door right after Ernestine. She headed straight for the counter and plopped onto a stool, telling Ernestine to come sit by her. "Make us two large root beer floats, Billie," Ada Jane ordered in her bossiest voice. Then she spun around on the stool at least ten times, until I wondered when she would get dizzy enough to fall off. "You need to hurry up," she said, "because Ernestine's mom is taking us swimming real soon."

"Too bad," I said, settling back into my chair. "We're fresh out of root beer."

Ada Jane turned to glare at me, and Ernestine made devil horns behind her head. Tommy laughed so hard he shot spit all over the table.

"We're out of what?" Mama said from the kitchen door.

"Billie won't wait on me, Mrs. Hughes," Ada Jane whined. "She says you're out of root beer. I've never heard of a diner running out of root beer before."

For a split second I saw something in Mama's eyes, like a laugh wanting to happen. But the door opened, and a group of men came in. "Billie," Mama said, "get up right now and serve Ada Jane. I'm going to wait on these folks."

I kept my back to Ada Jane while I made the floats, dumping two measly scoops of vanilla ice cream into her mug, then three heaping ones into Ernestine's. A pepper shaker just happened to be sitting at my fingertips, so I added four good shakes into Ada Jane's float. I topped it off with a squirt of whipped cream and a cherry on top.

"Here." I slammed her drink on the counter. "That'll be fifty cents for both of them." She pulled a crumpled one-dollar bill out of her pocket and threw it at me. I counted back fifty pennies to her. "Sorry," I said. "Mama forgot to get quarters."

Ada Jane put the pennies in her pocket like she couldn't care less. She sucked a mouthful of root beer through her straw and made a face. "No offense, Billie, but your floats aren't near as good as the ones in Millerstown."

Ernestine took a drink of hers. "Mmm. Mine's delicious."

"Maybe there's something wrong with your taste buds," I said to Ada Jane.

"Yeah," Tommy piped up. "You might have taste-bud-a-ria."

Ernestine's face turned pink, and I knew she was trying not to laugh. "Uh . . . B-B-Billie," she stammered, winking at me. "Can I see your pencil?"

"What do you need a pencil for?" Ada Jane said.

"Oh, nothing," Ernestine said. "I just want to draw something on my napkin."

And then Ada Jane, being the biggest copycat in the world, said she wanted a pencil, too. So they sat there drinking their floats and doodling on napkins. Before they left, Ernestine slipped me hers. "Read. It," she mouthed.

Tommy and I hurried back to the kitchen where I unfolded the napkin: "B and T. I think A.J. has the church money. I'm going to try and find it. Your friend, E."

Chapter 21

Daddy and Uncle Warren had outsmarted the cops. They were due back at the cabin in four days to pick up their car.

I found out about it July 3, when my uncles, Russell and Gary, came to the diner for Mama's special patriotic breakfast.

The day hadn't started too good. I'd been so busy with customers I barely had time to talk with Ernestine when she'd rushed in to give me an update on Ada Jane. She'd managed to sneak to the diner two times since last Thursday—to fill me in on her search for the money—but she'd never been able to stay more than a minute or so. Today she had a new plan. "I still haven't found anything," she'd whispered in my ear, "but I'm going to look inside you-know-who's closet. I've got a hunch that's where she's hiding it."

And then Castor Oil and Chipmunk Cheeks had

showed up, ordering two of Mama's biscuits and gravy specials. I could hardly stand to wait on them the way they kept bragging how the cops were closing in on Daddy and Uncle Warren. I was in the kitchen filling their plates when Denny whistled real loud and Bud said, "That's right. Captain of the Indy force says he's got an informant on the street who's heard some stuff. Guess one of them was spotted a few days ago."

What I wanted to do was go after that pepper shaker I'd used on Ada Jane's float and dump the whole thing over their biscuits. Instead, I settled for a pinch of the corn-starch Mama had left sitting out, then covered it over with gravy. I didn't get to see their expressions when they took that first bite, though, because Aunt Charlene delivered their plates. She'd been helping us out with the patriotic breakfast and said she wanted to be the one to serve Bud and Denny.

The good news didn't come until Castor Oil and his sidekick left the diner. That's when my uncles showed up.

Mama finally let me have a break, and I was in my corner booth eating sausage and a waffle. I'd leaned down to pick up a piece of sausage I'd dropped on the floor when my uncles Russell and Gary slid into the booth next to mine. I guess they hadn't noticed me, because right off the bat Uncle Russell started talking in a real low voice. "So you think you'll have it ready to go by this Saturday, huh?"

"No problem-o," Uncle Gary said. "Just got a little transmission work left. I'll have that baby ready to make it cross-country, count on it. You said they're hitting the road Sunday afternoon, right?"

"That's the word," Uncle Russell said. "They can't stay more than a night out there. Earl says Hinshaw's a nutcase. Says if they stay any longer, he'll likely wig out on 'em."

"Man, that old guy's one brick short of a load," Uncle Gary said. "They're smart to get the heck out of Dodge."

I'd been scrunched under the table the whole time they were talking, too excited to even swallow the waffle in my mouth. Daddy was going to be at the cabin on Sunday!

I slipped out of the booth, careful to keep my head turned and not attract my uncles' attention, and hurried back to the kitchen.

Mama was just hanging up the telephone. I grabbed the potato peeler and headed to the sink, my heart feeling like it might leap out of my throat. I tried not to act jumpy, though. I didn't want her getting suspicious.

"That was Joe," Mama said, looking all gooey-eyed. "He's got plans for the weekend. He wants to take us to Polly County for that Civil War reenactment, and then we'll spend Saturday night at a motel. He says to tell you it's got a swimming pool." Her lips stretched into a smile. "Won't that be fun, honey?"

She might as well have punched me in the nose. I couldn't even answer; I just stared at her with my mouth open.

I couldn't go to any Civil War reenactment, not over the weekend. Sunday was the only day I had to find Daddy.

I wanted to scream. Good old Joe Hughes was at it again, messing in my business. Of all the times to pick for a trip, how come he chose this weekend? And how could Mama stand there with that big smile on her face, acting so excited about a weekend away with Daddy Joe and a field full of cannons?

"I don't want to go," I finally managed to say. "Can't I stay with Aunt Charlene and Tommy?"

"Absolutely not. You're going with us."

"That's not fair!" I flung the potato peeler in the sink. Her and Daddy Joe were going to ruin everything. It'd be all their fault if Daddy got caught before I found him. "You just don't trust me. You still think Tommy and I stole that money."

"Keep your voice down, Billie. We've got customers out there."

"I don't care about any customers! I don't care about any stupid Civil War, either. All I want is to find Daddy and get away from you." I backed into the wall, already sorry for what I'd said. Big sobs heaved up my chest. I buried my eyes in my hands. Everything in my life had gone so wrong, I wished I could just slip down the drain with the dirty dishwater.

I wanted Mama to put her arms around me, to say she believed me, to say how sorry she was, and that I could stay home this weekend. Instead, she started working on an onion—chop, chop, chop—cutting it into a thousand little cubes. "I'd like to think you're telling the truth. But you two were caught red-handed. If that money you had wasn't from the church, then where did it come from?" Her eyes beamed in on mine. "I want to know, and I want the truth."

"Can I go home now?"

"No. Billie, I said I want the truth. Your Daddy Joe and I think you're hiding something."

"He . . . ain't . . . my . . . daddy. And I don't want to go anywhere with him this weekend."

Mama set the knife down and looked at me again, her eyes softening. "What is it, honey? Why do you still resent Joe so much? He just wants to do something nice for you and Carla."

"Because he's the reason Daddy left, that's why. He wanted you to himself, so he fired Daddy from Firestone on purpose. And then Daddy couldn't find another job. That's why he had to go to California." There. I'd finally said it.

Mama sighed, shaking her head. "I don't know where on God's earth you got that idea, Billie. It couldn't be further from the truth. I'm going to give it to you straight: Joe fired your dad because he stole equipment from the company. And I divorced him because he gambled all of our money away, then chased off to California after God knows what, probably something in a skirt. He left me alone—broke—with two children to feed."

I felt another sob bubbling at the bottom of my chest. How could Mama say that? She was wrong. I knew she was wrong. Daddy never had another girlfriend. "I love your Mama," he'd told me after he came back from California. "She's always been the one for me."

"That's not true," I said to Mama. "He went out there to work a special construction job with Uncle Gary. He told me so."

"He's told you a lot of stories, Billie. I'm sorry to say it, because I know how much you love your daddy. And in his own way, Earl loves you. But that doesn't make him a good father. A good father wouldn't leave his family. A good father wouldn't run out and rob a bank, causing his daughter this much pain."

"It was because of Uncle Warren he robbed the bank," I said. "Uncle Russell said so. He said Uncle Warren got into a bad mess, that he owed money to someone and was in a lot of trouble."

"It doesn't matter who owed what to who," Mama said. "What matters is that Earl made his own choices. The man's never grown up. Can't you understand that?"

I understood it, all right. She hated Daddy. I stood against the wall, my arms crossed, my teeth clamped together.

"Joe cares about you and Carla," she said, "like a father should. It's about time you started to appreciate him."

She stuck a spoon in her potato salad and swung back into the dining room. I followed her, stomping around the tables and out the front door, slamming it behind me. I figured she was too busy to chase after me.

I was sitting on Fuzzy's bench, wiping my eyes, when Aunt Charlene came outside. "What's wrong, honey?" she said.

"Nothing." I didn't feel like going into it all again.

She sat next to me and put her arm around my shoulders. "Sometimes life ain't all that easy, is it?"

I shook my head.

"It's pretty rough going now," she said. "Things will get better, though; they always do. Lord knows, I've had my share of troubles over the years. But one thing you've got going for you, hon, is a family that cares." She nudged me in the side and winked. "Even the one guy you're not so wild about."

"He ain't my daddy."

"I guess he'd like to give it a try," Aunt Charlene said, "if you'd let him."

I rested my head on her shoulder, still fighting the urge to cry. How could I give Joe Hughes a chance at anything when it was all his fault I wouldn't be looking for Daddy on Sunday?

Chapter 22

The next evening I sat between Tommy and Carla at the Myron baseball diamond, watching Fourth of July fireworks explode in the sky. I'd been chewing on my knuckles for the past half hour, still trying to come up with a scheme for the weekend. Tommy hadn't been any help, even when I'd told him our dads would be at the cabin on Sunday. I had the feeling he was secretly glad about Daddy Joe's weekend plans.

Carla clutched her ears and whooped when the night lit up with color. She snuggled against Daddy Joe, then crawled onto his lap and stuffed her Raggedy Andy doll into his shirt pocket. It dangled upside down by a cloth leg.

I watched them from the corner of my eye, remembering the last time I went to the fireworks with my real daddy. It seemed like a hundred years ago. I pushed the thought out of my mind and moved two rows down, where I didn't have to look at them anymore. Tommy followed me. It turned out we'd parked ourselves right behind Ernestine and Ada Jane.

"You'd better stop that," Ada Jane said when my knee accidentally jabbed her back. She spun around and scrunched her eyes at me. "I'm telling my grandma if you don't."

I flicked a crumb off the bleacher into her hair. "Go ahead. Tell your dumb old grandma anything you want. Tell her to go sit her big, fat butt on a tack."

I could've sworn I heard Ernestine swallow a giggle. Tommy cracked up laughing, spitting root beer on his shorts. "Yeah, tell her to go sit on a whole box of tacks," he said. "Maybe it'll let all the air out of her butt. Maybe she'll win a prize for letting out the world's biggest fart."

Ada Jane scooted down the bleachers, away from us. "Come on, Ernestine, let's go. I don't want to catch any cooties from you know who," she said.

Ernestine looked back at me, chomping her gum a million miles a minute. She winked a bunch of times like something was up.

"You got any more of that gum?" Tommy asked.

"Hurry up, Ernestine," Ada Jane said. "You know we ain't allowed to hang around them. And don't give him any of that gum—it's mine. I'm the one that bought it for you." By now Ada Jane had moved to the end of the bleachers, but she was still watching over her shoulder, tapping her fingers on the metal seat.

Ernestine's green eyes glowed bright as the moon. Her hair had slipped out of its ponytail and hung in long, tangled curls around her face, just like always. She turned her head so Ada Jane couldn't see her, then crossed her eyes and stuck her tongue out. I laughed out loud. Ernestine's goofiness made me ache for the time when we did everything together, just her, me, and Tommy. These days I could hardly get her alone for one second, not even long enough to tell her the news about Daddy.

Tommy unwrapped the piece of gum she handed him. "I've got to tell you something," I whispered.

Ernestine's eyes darted to Ada Jane, then back to me. "And I've got to tell *you* something," she said. "You guys meet me on your bikes behind the Polar Meat Locker tomorrow at noon. I'll tell you then."

When she turned to leave, something crossed my mind. A plan. "Wait," I said.

"Hurry *up*, Ernestine," Ada Jane snapped.

Ernestine looked from me to Ada Jane, then back to me. "What?"

"Are you lighting candles with Ada Jane at church Sunday?"

She nodded. "Why?"

"Can I take your place?" I asked, not believing my own ears.

"For real? With Ada Jane?"

"Yeah."

"What for?" Tommy said. "I thought you hated being an acolyte, especially with her."

"Never mind," I said. "I just need to, that's all."

"Sure," Ernestine said, and then she was gone, racing toward the concession stand with Ada Jane.

Ernestine had found the church money, I was sure of it. But if I couldn't get to Daddy on Sunday, it wouldn't matter one bit, even if we told on Ada Jane. Because then Castor Oil would start asking questions, like where the money Tommy and I were caught with had come from.

I had to meet Ernestine tomorrow; I had to warn her not to say anything about the money—even if she'd found it.

I started back up the bleachers to Mama. Somehow, I had to get on her good side. I had to make my plan work. I took her hand, fiddling with the diamond ring Daddy Joe had given her. "I'm real sorry about yesterday," I said. "What I said wasn't nice. I didn't mean it, I promise."

She swept a lock of hair from my eyes. "That's very mature of you to apologize, honey."

"But I still can't go to Polly County," I said. "I can't help it. Ada Jane just reminded me it's my Sunday to light the church candles. Ernestine did it last week, and Ada Jane said there ain't no one else to ask. I'd forgotten all about it."

"Maybe you can trade weeks," Mama said. "I'll talk to Mirabelle."

"No, that won't work," I said, my heart racing faster with every word. "I'm already signed up and everything."

Daddy Joe's deep voice took me by surprise. "It's good to see you're taking this commitment seriously," he said. "If you're on the schedule to light candles, I don't want to interfere with it. We'll plan something for another weekend."

"Thanks," I said, then turned my head and let out a long stream of air. I'd done it! And for once Daddy Joe's nosing in my business had paid off. I took a deep breath and crossed my fingers: I had one more thing to take care of with Mama. "Can I ride bikes with Tommy and Ernestine tomorrow? Please. Just for a little while."

"Where?" Mama said, raising her eyebrows.

"Around town. Ernestine asked us."

"You miss her, don't you?"

I nodded, trying to look as pathetic as possible.

"Okay, I'm going to let you. You've worked hard the last two weeks. I'll talk to Charlene about it. But I don't want to hear the first word about any trouble."

I grinned from ear to ear, giving Mama a hug as the last of the fireworks boomed above us.

On the walk home Daddy Joe lit sparklers for everyone. Carla pouted when her two burned out, so he gave her an extra one, which meant she got more than I did. Like usual, he favored her over me; she always got the extra when something was uneven.

I waved my sparkler in big circles, remembering the last Fourth of July fireworks I'd gone to with my real daddy, just three years ago. He'd given us kids at least fifty sparklers apiece. It'd taken us a whole hour to burn them up.

"Where'd you get all those sparklers?" Mama had asked him. She had a doubtful look on her face, like she suspected funny business.

"Courtesy of the Lions Club," Daddy answered, grinning at me. "They'll never miss them."

"You mean you took—"

"Now don't get your bowels in an uproar," Daddy had joked. "They had a whole crate of them. It's no big deal. Russell got some, too."

But Mama wouldn't let up. "You've got to pay for them, Earl," she'd said later.

"Uh . . . yeah, sure," Daddy had promised. "I'll get down there tomorrow and take care of it."

"Watch out, Billie!" Carla yelled, startling me out of my daydream. She was twirling in circles, whipping her last sparkler around like a sword. She nearly caught my blouse on fire.

"Whoa there! Better watch where you're walking, Billie," Daddy Joe said. "I don't want you kids to get burned."

Well, here we go again, I thought. First he gives Carla the extra sparkler, and then he tells me to watch where I'm walking. Couldn't he see it was Carla's fault? And who did he think he was kidding; he didn't want me to get burned? I bet he wouldn't care one bit if I smoldered into a heap of ashes right there in the middle of the sidewalk. The only thing Daddy Joe cared about was hogging all of Mama's attention. He'd had his long octopus arms wrapped around her half the night.

I slowed down to walk beside Tommy. "I can't go with you and Ernestine tomorrow," he said. "I ain't got a bike anymore." He trapped a lightning bug between the palm of his hands, peeking through his fingers at it.

"Let's go get it." The words popped out of my mouth so fast they surprised even me.

"What? You mean go over to Goble's house? We can't do that."

"Why not? It's your bike, ain't it? It's not like we're stealing it."

"I'm not allowed out. My mom would kill me if she

found out I snuck over to the Watsons'." Tommy eyed Aunt Charlene like he was afraid she'd heard him, but her and Bud Castor were several feet ahead of us, walking side by side. They were plastered together tighter than Band-Aids, hooting with laughter about some joke Bud had just told.

Tommy jerked his thumb toward them and whispered, "Castor Oil's over at my place all the time now. What if him and my mom catch me sneaking out?"

"They'll never know. They aren't going to look in your bedroom. Besides, we'll wait until after everyone goes to bed."

He darted after another lightning bug, missing it by a mile.

"You aren't scared, are you?" I said.

"Who said I'm scared?" He stopped on the sidewalk, socking a fist into his hand. "I'd like to get hold of that scumbag Goble, just once. He ain't as tough as he thinks he is."

A half hour later Tommy and I stood in the street, staring at the run-down house where Goble Watson lived with his six brothers and sisters and their loudmouthed mother. Even though it'd been my idea, I was already worried about sneaking out. If Mama caught me, she'd never let me out of the house tomorrow. But then I reminded myself she could sleep through a hurricane. I'd closed my bedroom door, just in case Daddy Joe got up during the night. If only Carla didn't wake up, I'd be safe. Besides, it's not like we were doing anything wrong. All we wanted was to get Tommy's bike back. Goble didn't have any right to keep it.

A shiver slid down my spine when I saw the Watsons' German shepherd chained to a tree by the side of the house. He had some kind of bone on the ground in front of him, but he looked up and bared his teeth at us. A long, low growl rumbled in the back of his throat.

We didn't see Tommy's bike anywhere in the front yard, but truthfully, it would've been hard to find anything in that junk heap. Broken toys, rusted tools, lamps without shades, and garbage cans were flung all over the place. A wringer washing machine sat at the bottom of the porch steps with weeds growing out of it, and a sign that said NITE CRAWLERS 4 SALE was taped to its side. I counted seven cars parked in the middle of the yard, some with their hoods open, one of them missing all its doors.

We made a wide circle around the dog and headed toward the backyard. We were crouched beside a shed when I spotted something under a pile of automobile parts near the house. It looked like the spokes of a bike wheel. I crept closer, trying to get a better look. Sure enough, Tommy's bike was at the bottom of the pile. Under the light of the moon we started tossing stuff aside, until Tommy finally wrestled his bike free. He pulled it upright.

"Hop on the fender," he said.

But just as I went to swing my leg over, a shrill cry came from under the bike.

"Look!" Tommy said. He stooped to pick up a yellow ball of fluff. "It's a kitten. I must've run over its tail." The kitten cocked its head at him and mewed pathetically. "Aw . . . ain't it cute?" he said.

Tommy started to tickle the kitten's chin, but the dog went crazy barking, and we heard voices coming from the front yard. He dropped the kitten into his bike basket, then started off with me on the fender. It didn't take but a couple of seconds to realize we weren't going anywhere on his bicycle. The front tire was flat.

"Oh, man," Tommy muttered, but he wasn't talking about the tire. "It's Goble's mom."

We tore out of the yard—not before she'd seen us, though. "Someone's out back, Goble!" she hollered. "Let the dog loose."

We must've cut through ten more yards before the yelling and barking finally faded away. By now I had the kitten, because the bike was bouncing around so much it'd almost flown out of the basket. We turned down a dark alley and followed it another block before venturing onto a sidewalk.

Tommy stopped under the streetlight, trying to catch his breath. "Looks like we ditched them," he said.

I collapsed next to him. He reached down and took the kitten from me, cradling it like a baby, cooing in its face. "Aw, man," he said. "I love this little thing. I'm keeping it."

While Tommy cuddled the kitten, I started thinking about Sunday again, about finding Daddy. "You know,"

I said, "we'll have to leave first thing after church on Sunday. If we wait too late, we'll miss them. Uncle Russell says they're pulling out in the afternoon." I'd already been over this with Tommy at least ten times, but he never seemed to pay that much attention.

"I hope it doesn't have worms," he said, touching noses with the kitten. "Worms can kill them, you know."

"What're you talking about? Didn't you hear me?"

"Yeah, I heard you."

"Well, I'm going out there Sunday morning. Are you coming with me or not?"

He buried his face in the kitten's soft fur. I'd never seen him act so crazy over an animal. "I ain't sure. Maybe."

"Maybe? That's all you've got to say, after you promised me? Don't you want to see our dads? Don't you want them to come back and tell everyone the truth about the money?"

"Aw, come on. That's stupid. You know they ain't going to do that."

His flat, lifeless voice drained the hope right out of me. I wanted to yell at him, to tell him how wrong he was. I wanted to tell him how my daddy would do anything in the world for me, even if his own dad wouldn't. I couldn't say it, though. I couldn't say anything, because all of a sudden the *crunch, crunch, crunch* of footsteps froze my voice in my throat.

Then three shadowy figures slid out of the alley and surrounded us.

A hand reached out for Tommy's kitten.

Chapter 23

Tommy jerked away from Goble, clutching the kitten to his chest. "Keep your—"

Goble shoved him. Tommy fell backward on top of his bike, losing his grip on the kitten. It flipped into the spokes of his wheel. He grabbed for it, but one of the Etchison twins beat him to it. The twin snatched the kitten by the tail, dangling it upside down and laughing.

"Stop that!" I lunged at him and dug my fingernails in his arm, trying to make him drop the kitten. The other twin pushed me away, making me fall on top of Tommy. He scrambled out from under me, rose to his knees, and glared up at Goble.

"You'd better leave that kitten alone."

"Or what, sissy boy?" Goble stood over us, his face smeared with meanness. "Are you gonna cry about the itty-bitty kitty?"

I spat at his feet. "Ugly turd."

"Shut up, Wisher, before we wring your stupid cat's neck." Goble kicked my leg. It felt like he'd crushed a bone, but I didn't cry out. I didn't want to give him the satisfaction.

Tommy hopped up and faced him, his chest heaving. "What do you want? We ain't done nothing to you." He looked at the kitten, his eyes glistening with tears.

Goble snorted. "You shouldn't have come messing around my house. I warned you not to. I want the bike back."

Goble snapped his finger, and the Etchison twin tossed the kitten to him like it was a baseball. Goble squeezed the little thing, making it cry again. He shook it over Tommy's head. Then, before I even saw it coming, Tommy socked Goble in the gut.

Goble clutched his stomach with his free hand. "You punk. You're gonna pay for that. This cat ain't never gonna live to—"

"Give me the cat." A gruff voice from the street caused me to snap my head around. Daddy Joe stood behind me, looking taller than the streetlamp. He took three quick steps and grabbed Goble by the scruff of his neck. Goble's mouth fell open, and without a word, he handed Daddy Joe the kitten. The Etchison twins backed away slowly, then swung around at the very same time and ran down the alley.

"What's going on here? You threatening these kids?" Daddy Joe held the kitten in one hand and Goble in the other.

"They was snooping around my house. I heard they stole some money from the church. I was just checking to make sure they ain't got nothing of mine," Goble whimpered.

"Liar! You're the thief." I shoved Goble's arm. "You took Tommy's bike the other night. We were just going after it. If you don't watch out, I'm going to—"

"I'll talk to you in a minute, young lady," Daddy Joe said in a stern voice. He lifted Goble straight up off his feet and gave him a good shake. "I ever hear of you picking on these two again or taking their bikes, you're going to be one sorry fellow. You got that?"

Goble nodded, squirming like a worm while Daddy Joe held on to him.

"Now get out of here. I don't want you anywhere near these kids again."

I didn't say anything the whole way home. Tommy did all the talking. You would've thought he'd beat the snot out of

Goble the way he bragged and carried on. Daddy Joe listened and nodded, answering every once in a while with an "uh-huh."

I walked a few feet behind them, sweating up a storm, wondering how it was that Daddy Joe had turned up in the middle of the night. I'd thought he was asleep when I left the house earlier, but now I suspected he'd been spying on me.

We were almost home when he spotted Carla's Raggedy Andy doll on the sidewalk. He stooped to pick it up. "I've been looking everywhere for this," he said. "Carla dropped it on the way home from the fireworks. I couldn't sleep, so I thought I'd venture out and track it down."

My heart pattered in my chest. Was Daddy Joe telling the truth, or had he been following us all along? One thing I knew for sure: if he told Mama about finding me in a fight with Goble Watson, she'd never let me leave the house again.

We dropped Tommy off at home with his new pet. "I'm calling her Tiger, because she's so tough," he said after Daddy Joe told him it was a girl. He waved good-night to us, then slipped inside his trailer and closed the door, cooing softly at the kitten.

That left me with Daddy Joe. Alone. I dreaded it. I didn't want to answer any questions, so I hurried across the street ahead of him.

"Billie."

I sped up.

"Billie, come here."

I knew I had to face him. I turned around, and for the first time ever, I begged him for something. "Please, please don't tell Mama I snuck out."

"Never mind about that now. Did that Watson kid hurt you?"

"Just my leg. He kicked me."

"If you and Tommy wanted that bike back, why didn't you ask me?"

I shrugged. Even though he was standing right next to me, it seemed like the whole Pacific Ocean separated us. I couldn't say anything to him, because I didn't know the answer.

He knelt beside me, so we were eye to eye. "I won't tell your mother, Billie. This time. But don't try anything like that again. Ever. Understand? This is your last warning. And you come to me the next time you need help, okay?"

"Okay," I said, then hurried inside. What did he mean, come to him if I needed help? Did he really think I'd let him nose into my business?

I had a hard time falling asleep that night. My mind raced in every direction. I worried Daddy Joe wouldn't keep his word about not telling Mama I'd snuck out. And of course, I thought about Daddy. Would he really be at the cabin on Sunday, like Uncle Russell had said?

I had another thought, too, just as I drifted off to sleep. About what'd happened three years ago on the Fourth of July, with Daddy and the sparklers. Had he ever gone back and paid the Lions Club for them?

The next morning I avoided Mama and Daddy Joe as much as possible. When I met up with Tommy, I quizzed him about whether Aunt Charlene had heard him come in. "Naw," he said. "She was sound asleep snoring."

We worked like maniacs cleaning the church kitchen. I wanted to be sure to get out of there by noon to meet Ernestine, so I scrubbed everything until it shone. I couldn't believe it when Mirabelle inspected the sink and said what a good job I'd done.

"You're finally getting the knack of this. I'm going to talk to your moms about keeping you after your punishment ends. I could use a couple of helpers around here." She tore open a sack of cookies and gave each of us two.

After she left the kitchen, Tommy pulled Tiger out of a box he'd hidden in the closet. He'd been sneaking milk to her every ten minutes or so.

"You're going to make her sick," I said when he opened the icebox for the hundredth time.

"Nuh-uh. This is just what she needs. Milk's the best thing for her." He sounded like he was all of a sudden an expert on cats or something. "Besides, she's nearly starved to death. Just look at how skinny she is." He held her up for me to see.

When we got home, Tommy's bike was leaning against our front porch with both tires pumped up. He hid Tiger back in his bedroom—he still hadn't asked Aunt Charlene if he could keep her—and we took off downtown to meet Ernestine.

It wasn't noon yet, so we decided to kill some time and look around Clarksons'.

"Maybe they have a bigger box I can use for Tiger," Tommy said.

We were walking toward the back of the store to ask Mr. Clarkson about the box when I heard Mrs. Clarkson in the next aisle. "Just where do you think you're going with that doll, young lady?" she said.

"She was going to leave with it. I saw her take it out of the box, Mrs. Clarkson." That was Ada Jane talking. I could've recognized her whiny voice from a mile away.

"Is that right?" Mrs. Clarkson said. "I suspected as much. You say she was leaving with it?"

"Yes, ma'am. I saw her, too," Lou Ann said.

"Give that doll to me right now," Mrs. Clarkson snapped. "We'll go have a word with your mother."

"No, I ain't giving it back! I'm buying it."

Carla!

Chapter 24

Tommy and I raced to the end of the aisle and turned down the next one. Carla was standing in the toy section with her back against the wall and a giant Kimmy doll clutched tight to her chest. Ada Jane, Rhonda, and Lou Ann were standing around her, giggling.

Mrs. Clarkson's hand whipped out like a lizard's tongue, snatching the doll by its leg. She gave it a good yank. Carla kept hold of its hair and tugged back furiously, but then she saw me. She let go of the doll and ran to me, crying, "Tell her, Billie! Tell her I'm buying it."

"Golly day, Mrs. Clarkson," Ada Jane said, her voice sweet like persimmon pudding, "it sure didn't look like she was buying that doll to us. Did it, Rhonda?"

"Nuh-uh. She just ripped it right out of its box," Rhonda said. "I thought she was going to leave with it."

"Me too," Lou Ann said. "Besides, she doesn't even have money."

"Yes, I do!" Carla wailed, pulling a crumpled bill from her pocket. "See? I've got five dollars right here. It's mine; I found it." I clenched my teeth when she waved Abraham Lincoln in front of our faces. That was my money! She'd taken it from the drawer. I wanted to snatch it out of her hand, but I couldn't make myself do it in front of Mrs. Clarkson.

"Just where did you *find* that money, young lady?" Mrs. Clarkson said.

"Under Billie's socks," Carla said, her voice cracking. "But it's finders keepers, so it's mine now. Ain't that right, Billie?"

I swallowed my anger and put my arm around her. "She's telling the truth," I said to Mrs. Clarkson, staring her straight in the eye. "That's my birthday money, but I'm giving it to Carla. She can buy the doll if she wants."

I'd scold her later for taking my money. But for now I just wanted to get us out of the store. After we'd finally paid for the Kimmy doll and left, I took the change and sent Carla across the street to the diner.

"Jeez," Tommy said. "I didn't know you got five whole dollars for your birthday. Man, that's a lot of money."

Ada Jane and her friends were standing a few feet down the sidewalk, snickering. "Ha! Betcha anything that's not birthday money. Betcha it's church money," Rhonda said.

"Unless it's from her daddy," Lou Ann said. "And we know where he got it, don't we?"

Ada Jane squealed. "Eew! That means it was touched by a *real live crook.*"

"Well, it takes one to know one, doesn't it, turd?" I said to Ada Jane. I picked my bike up from the sidewalk and pushed it out to the street.

"Yeah," Tommy said. "It takes one to know one."

"You'd better quit cussing at me, Billie Wisher, or I'm telling your mother," Ada Jane yelled as we sped away.

We found Ernestine in the alley behind the Polar Meat Locker, standing next to a truckload of hogs. My insides felt queasy when I realized it was Saturday, the day farmers hauled their livestock to the locker to have them slaughtered and butchered. I turned my head when I walked by the back entrance, but not before I saw a fat pink pig swinging from a rope.

"How come you wanted to meet back here?" I asked Ernestine, trying to ignore the pig's squeals.

"Because I didn't want you know who to see me." Ernestine reached in her pocket and pulled out some gum, handing me and Tommy a piece. She nodded her head toward the hog truck. "Miss Prissy would never come back here looking for me." She pinched her nose and crinkled her eyes, imitating Ada Jane. "Ooh . . . piggies! They're so . . . ooh . . . icky!"

Tommy and I cracked up, and all of a sudden it seemed like old times again. We walked our bikes down the alley where Ernestine could tell us her news.

"Guess what?" she said. Her eyes sparkled with excitement. "I was right. Ada Jane's the one who took the money. I found it."

"Holy cow! You mean you really found the church money?" Tommy said.

Ernestine grinned. "Yep."

"Was it in her closet?" I asked.

"Yep."

"How'd you know she took it?" Tommy said.

"I suspected her all along," Ernestine said. "Especially when she kept on buying things and hiding them so her mom wouldn't see. She acted like her grandma Mirabelle had given her money, but I knew she was making it up."

"How'd you find it?" Tommy said.

"I snooped in her closet while she was in the bathroom. I saw an envelope sticking out of a shoe. It looked just like the one her grandpa gave her to put in the church office, like the one you guys had." Ernestine looked over her shoulder, then leaned closer to Tommy and me, her hands cupped around her mouth. "There was *gobs* of money in it."

"You didn't tell anyone yet, did you?" I said, my mouth starting to feel dry.

Ernestine's face fell. "No. Because now it's gone again."

"What do you mean, it's gone again?" Tommy said. "Why didn't you take the money out of the closet? You could've proved we didn't swipe it."

"I wanted to but then Ada Jane came back in her room looking for me. The next time I had a chance to get it, it was gone."

"Aw, man," Tommy said. "We'll never be able to prove anything now."

"It doesn't matter," I said, trying to make Ernestine feel better. "We couldn't have told on her yet anyway. We have to wait until after we see our dads on Sunday." My heart pounded just saying those words.

Ernestine's eyes grew three times their size. "You're seeing your dads on Sunday? You mean you're going back out to crazy Old Man Hinshaw's again. For real?" She pulled her gum into a long strand and wrapped it around her pinkie finger, staring at us the whole time. "How come you want to do that?"

"I ain't the one who said I wanted to go," Tommy said. He looked at the ground, making grooves in the gravel with his bare toes.

I knew Tommy didn't want to go out to the cabin again. He'd made that clear. But I did, more than anything. I had lots of reasons to find Daddy. I'd been thinking about it ever since I'd first heard about the robbery. For one thing, I wanted him to tell me why he'd done it: was it really like I'd heard, that Uncle Warren had to pay money back to gangsters? I wanted to know where Daddy was going, too, or if I'd ever see him again. I wanted him to come back to Myron and turn himself in, then tell Bud Castor the truth about the money I'd found. I wanted to hear him say to everyone, "My girl didn't steal this money. I did."

I tried to explain all this to Ernestine and Tommy. Nothing came out right, though. I sputtered and stumbled over my words, making everything sound all jumbled up. I could tell they didn't understand what I was talking about. I felt like shouting, "How come you don't get it?"

I slid down the side of the building, feeling more helpless than the poor, squealing pig. "I have to find him. I just have to." I buried my face in my hands.

Ernestine sat beside me. "Don't cry, Billie."

"I ain't crying," I said, swallowing my sniffles.

"Hey," she said, taking my hand, "I'll go with you. I'll help you find your dad."

"You will? Really?"

"Cross my heart."

Tommy slid down next to us. "Aw, heck. I'll go, too. I ain't scared of Old Man Hinshaw."

We planned it all out then. Once we got over the bridge, Ernestine would hide by the wooded lane and be our lookout. That way she could come running to warn us if she saw Old Man Hinshaw or anyone else prowling around. Tommy and I would go on to the cabin to find our dads. I'd do all of the talking because Tommy said he didn't want to. I agreed to that and thought we had it all settled, except right when we went to shake on it, Tommy chickened out about going with me inside the cabin.

"Maybe I should stay outside," he said. "We'll probably need two lookouts, just in case Old Man Hinshaw comes at us from another direction."

I didn't argue with him this time; I was just happy they both were going with me. We decided to head out the first thing after church on Sunday. That was only two days away.

There wasn't a doubt in my mind I'd find Daddy. I should've felt excited, especially since he could finally tell Bud Castor the truth. But a chill swept over me when I hopped on my bike. Would Daddy really do what I wanted him to?

Chapter 25

I woke up Sunday morning to the *snip, snip, snip* of scissors. A pile of freshly cut doll's hair sat next to my pillow.

"Lookee here." Carla's voice bubbled with excitement as she shoved the Kimmy doll in my face. "I'm giving her a pixie cut. Ain't it cute?"

I had to hold back my laughter. She'd chopped the doll's hair into a bunch of uneven layers, until all it had left for bangs were some short stubs that stuck straight up.

"You know her hair won't grow back, don't you?"

"Of course I know that. I ain't stupid." Carla tilted her head and scrunched her eyes, concentrating on the doll like she was getting ready to pull its tonsils out. She took a quick snip over its ear, leaving a big bald spot. "It don't matter if it's short anyways, 'cause I have a special hat she's going to wear to church this morning."

Church. I rolled my eyes with dread, remembering the

price I had to pay for getting out of the Civil War weekend with Daddy Joe. It meant lighting candles with Miss Prissy, then one whole hour of sitting between her and Whitey in the front church pew. I couldn't have dreaded anything worse, not even ten pages of arithmetic problems.

Mama was frying bacon in the kitchen. I put on the baby blue dress she'd bought me in April and my only white shoes that weren't scuffed up, then found my white gloves. Mirabelle made all of her acolytes wear gloves during the church service; she said it showed reverence to the Lord. I'd tried to tell her that wearing gloves made it too hard to turn the hymnal pages, but she'd snapped at me to hush, that some things just had to be endured.

"My goodness," Mama said when she saw me. She laid a piece of sizzling bacon on her platter, then took a step back and looked me over. "You look beautiful, honey, just like an angel. Doesn't she, Joe?"

Daddy Joe pulled his attention away from a newsmagazine and looked up at me. The way they both stared—all wide-eyed and admiring—you would've thought I'd just won first place at the National Spelling Bee.

I squirmed in my tight shoes, wishing Mama hadn't compared me to an angel; it made me itch with guilt to think how I was tricking her. The day before, I'd begged her and Aunt Charlene to let Tommy and me play dodgeball with some Sunday school kids after church, and they'd said okay. Except there wasn't going to be any dodgeball game; I'd made it all up.

I felt bad about the lie—real bad—but I wasn't about to change my plans now. Nothing could stop me from finding Daddy.

Carla called from the bedroom, wanting me to tie a hat over her Kimmy doll's bald head.

"That was mighty nice of you to buy your sister that doll with your birthday money," Daddy Joe said.

"It's okay," I muttered. "I didn't mind."

When Carla and I left for Sunday school, Mama called out the door that she might be there for church services, so she could watch me light candles. I figured the only reason she'd show up was to make sure I didn't set fire to Ada Jane. Mama hadn't ever been much for going to church, and I'd yet to see Daddy Joe set a foot inside one. It didn't seem fair they stayed home every week while I got stuck in Whitey Hudson's boring Sunday school classroom.

Carla made a big fuss of pulling the Kimmy doll in her wagon, the last thing in the world I wanted her to do. Mama hadn't made me go to church since Daddy robbed the bank, and I knew people were going to stare at me. That clunky doll was only going to attract more attention.

"You sure you want to take her?" I glanced back at the Kimmy doll as we rattled across the street. Its hat had fallen off already, and to tell the truth, the new hairdo looked like something Mama had run through her meat grinder. "What if everybody wants to hold her? Then you'll have to share."

I thought that would do the trick, but Carla just shook her head. "Nuh-uh. I ain't going to let no one pick her up but you."

We found Tommy behind his trailer playing with Tiger. "I'm teaching her to use the bathroom out here. Mom says I can't keep her if she doesn't quit doing her business inside." He took hold of the kitten's paws and scratched a little hole in some loose dirt, then cooed to her like he was talking to a baby.

"Be a good girl, Tiger. Wittle kitty go tinkle."

We waited for a while, but Tiger didn't seem interested in anything except chasing twigs around the grass. Carla scooped the kitten up in her arms, begging to play with it.

"You're still oing-gay you know where with me and Ernestine, aren't you?" I said, checking to make sure Carla hadn't caught on to my pig Latin. She'd already jumped on Tommy's tire swing and was spinning Tiger in circles.

From the look on Tommy's face, I could tell he'd rather spend the day with Mirabelle than go anywhere near that cabin. "We ook-shay on it, didn't we?" he grumbled, then turned his attention to Carla and the kitten.

I made a face at his back. He acted like he cared more about Tiger than he did our dads, or even me, for that matter. I paced around the yard, wondering why things had changed so much between us in the last couple of weeks. I remembered the day we'd first found out about the robbery, how he'd acted so full of himself, like our dads were movie stars. Now it seemed like he couldn't care less about them.

"We'll have to leave right after urch-chay," I said.

"What about the rain-tray?" Tommy said. "It nearly ran us over last time."

"It's Sunday."

"So what?"

"The trains don't run on Sunday." At least I didn't think they did. Funny, I thought, how all these years I'd been watching the trains, and now I couldn't remember if they ran on Sundays. I guess Tommy believed me, though, because he didn't argue about it.

It was just like I thought when we got to church. A crowd of bug-eyed kids stared at us as we walked up with Carla's noisy wagon. Ada Jane stood smack in the middle of them, wearing a frilly pink dress and pink bows in her hair. Tommy and I ignored her giggles and headed straight for the church door, but Carla stopped to show everyone her doll. "Look here, Ada Jane," she said. "I gave Kimmy a pixie cut."

Ada Jane smirked. "Oooh, what a funny hairstyle. It looks just like your sister's." She covered her mouth with her hand and giggled even louder.

Carla ran off to show her doll to her Sunday school friends, and I turned to face Ada Jane. "At least I don't look like a clown," I said.

"Well, at least I don't have a daddy that's wanted for bank robberies in three different states."

I stood speechless for a second, wishing I could yank the ruffles off Ada Jane's dress and stuff them down her throat.

"Liar," I said, my heart pounding. What did she mean, wanted for robberies in three states?

"Call me names if you want to. But I ain't lying. I heard so myself from my grandpa. He says there's going to be a reward out for anybody that catches both of your dads, because they're armed and dangerous and a menace to society. That's what Grandpa Whitey said. So there."

My head felt like it wanted to explode. I didn't know there was a reward out for Daddy and Uncle Warren. How come nobody had told me? I turned to Tommy; he looked as dumbfounded as me.

"Hey," one of the boys with Ada Jane said, "maybe

they'll put your dads' pictures up at the post office on the FBI's most wanted criminals list."

"You'd better cut it out," Tommy said. He drew his balled fist back. I worried he'd take a swing at someone like he did Goble, but the sight of Whitey Hudson lumbering up the steps sent Ada Jane and her friends scattering like ants.

Whitey didn't look so good: purple streaks and blotches covered his sweaty face, and his forehead gleamed with sweat. He pushed his thick glasses down to the tip of his nose and wiped his eyes with a handkerchief. Then he hunched over, grabbing the rail to steady himself. It seemed like every breath he took might be his last. I tried to slip away from him into the church foyer, but I wasn't quick enough.

He pulled himself upright and stuck out his hand, blocking me. "One minute there, Miss Billie Wisher." His voice sounded raspy and faint. "Not so fast. I wanted you to know Mirabelle washed and ironed them acolyte robes. One of them had gum stuck all over it— a real mess. They're clean now, though. They're hanging in the sanctuary closet."

"Thank you," I muttered, starting on my way again.

"You ain't chewin' any gum today, are you?"

"No. And it wasn't me who got gum on the robe."

Tommy and I walked through the sanctuary toward our Sunday school class, and I thought about Daddy hiding in the cabin, waiting to make a run for it. If what Ada Jane had said about the reward was true, wouldn't other people be out looking for them, too? I imagined everyone in Myron would want to get in on the action, even Goble Watson. I said a silent prayer, begging God to help me find Daddy first so I could warn him about everything. But I couldn't shake the feeling that God was mad at me, that something bad lurked around the corner.

We found Ernestine by herself in Whitey's classroom, reading comics that she'd hidden inside her lesson book.

She sucked in a gum bubble when she saw us, then hopped up and poked her head outside the classroom. "I'm hiding from Ada Jane," she said. "She makes me want to puke. She's already asked if I can come over after church, but I told her no. I hope she doesn't go and ask my mom."

When I started telling Ernestine what Ada Jane had just said, her eyes grew bigger and rounder by the second. "For real? There's really a reward out for your dads? That means a lot of people will be looking for them, huh?"

I chewed at my knuckles, dreading the thought of sitting in church for two more hours. I wished we were already on our way to Old Man Hinshaw's cabin.

Whitey shuffled into the room while we were talking. I stuck a pencil in my mouth and buried my face in my Sunday school workbook, hoping he wouldn't say anything to me. Ada Jane and her group piled in after him, and then Whitey rapped on his desk for attention. He opened his big white Bible.

"Boys and girls," he said, once everyone got settled, "in light of the special circumstances recently occurring in our community, we won't be studying our regular lesson today." He coughed a couple of times and continued. "I'm under the impression that a few of us could use a good, strong review of the Lord's laws, starting with the Ten Commandments." He coughed again and paused.

"In par-tic-u-lary," Whitey went on, "I'd like to focus

on the fifth commandment our Lord laid down." He smacked his Bible shut and looked straight at me. "Thou Shalt Not Steal. The fifth holy commandment." He was roaring by now, which caused another wheezing spell. He leaned over his desk, then took a shaky breath and said, "Billie Wisher, what do you think the Lord would tell us about that fifth commandment, Thou Shalt Not Steal?"

The room fell silent as a funeral parlor. Tommy fidgeted beside me. I sat up in my chair and looked Whitey Hudson square in the eye, my heart pounding so hard my chest hurt. "Well, I guess the Lord might tell you to study up on your commandments, because in my Bible, 'Thou Shalt Not Steal' ain't the fifth commandment, it's the eighth."

Whitey grabbed his desk, his face turning a solid shade of purple. A snicker started around the room, and before long it turned into roaring howls of laughter. Whitey tried to hush us, but no one paid him the slightest attention.

"You're going to get in big trouble," Ada Jane said over the laughter, pointing at me.

I didn't care. And I didn't care what happened to her, either. I stood up and yelled, "Oh, yeah? You're the one that's going to be in trouble, especially when your grandpa finds out what you took!"

Her face went white. She looked at Ernestine, then back at me. She started to say something, but we heard a soft thud, and someone yelled, "Something's wrong with your grandpa, Ada Jane!"

Ada Jane jerked her head toward the front of the room. She gasped, clamping her hand over her mouth. Whitey Hudson lay flat on the floor.

"He's dead!" Ada Jane screamed.

I ran to Whitey, looking helplessly at his limp body. I couldn't see his chest moving. "Call Reverend Clarkson," I yelled to Tommy. "Tell him we need an ambulance."

The next thing I knew a crowd of grown-ups flocked in the room and hovered over Whitey. Confusion broke out everywhere. Someone tried to get his pulse. Someone else struggled to get his tie off. Mirabelle went crazy, hollering at everyone to quit crowding him.

"It's just the asthma!" she kept yelling. "It's just the asthma acting up again. Give him air!"

After a couple of minutes us kids got whisked into the sanctuary. I stood with Ernestine and Tommy at the back of the room, chewing on the collar of my dress, praying Whitey would be okay. I'd never wanted him sick; I'd just wanted him to quit picking on me.

Ada Jane came storming toward us. "It's all your fault if my grandpa dies, Billie Wisher. You shouldn't have said none of that—it caused him to have a heart attack."

I backed out the door and raced down the steps, away from her accusing words. It's true, I thought, my heart aching with shame. This time I've gone and killed Whitey Hudson.

Chapter 26

I stood shivering at the bottom of the church steps, my arms wrapped tight around my chest. I wanted to run away, to not have to face Ada Jane or Mirabelle or anybody else at the church, but I couldn't. It wouldn't be right to leave until help came for Whitey.

I started pacing the sidewalk, watching for the ambulance. Surely it wouldn't take them long to get there. The Henderson County hospital was only a few miles from Myron.

It wasn't but a couple of minutes before Tommy and Ernestine came looking for me. I'd never seen Ernestine so mad.

"That stupid Ada Jane's in there telling everyone a bunch of lies," she said. Her eyes blazed in the bright sunlight.

"About me?"

"Uh . . ." Ernestine glanced at Tommy. He looked

straight down and kept his hands buried in his pockets, like he was studying a bug or something on the ground.

I tugged at his shirt sleeve. "What? What did she say?"

"Aw, she's just stupid. I swear I'm going to stuff a rag in her mouth one of these days." He picked up a rock from the sidewalk and sent it skipping across the street.

"She's a big, fat liar," Ernestine said. "I told her so, too."

"Will you just hurry up and tell me! I want to know what she said."

Ernestine bit her bottom lip and lowered her eyes. "She said your Daddy Joe's planning on sending you to reform school. She said him and Bud Castor and her grandpa have already called the school about it."

"Reform school?" I stumbled backward, covering my mouth with my hands. Is that what Mirabelle had meant the day after the robbery, the day I'd heard her say something about a school for juvenile delinquents?

"Don't mention that to Wanda," Daddy Joe had told her.

Was it true? Was Daddy Joe really planning to send me to reform school? Was Mama going along with him? Or maybe he was still trying to butter her up about it. And what about Tommy? They must be planning to send him away, too.

I pictured myself locked in a small gray room at the Indianapolis Girls' School, eating cold hominy grits for breakfast with nothing but a Bible to read. I'd never be let outside. I'd never get to have company. And I'd heard all the kids at reform school got whipped at least once a day.

"I should've told her to go stick her head in the toilet. I would've, too, if the preacher hadn't been standing there." Tommy kept talking, but I barely heard him. All I could hear were steel doors clanging behind me at reform school.

"Don't pay any attention to Ada Jane," Ernestine said. "Just wait until you find your real daddy. He won't let anyone send you away."

I nodded, feeling a little better. Ernestine was right; Daddy would make things okay. He'd never let Joe Hughes send me to reform school.

We heard the wail of a siren. A few people had trickled outside and gathered on the church steps, watching for the ambulance. It didn't take long before it bounced around the corner and screeched to a stop. Two men jumped out with a stretcher and hurried inside after Whitey. I sat down on the steps between Ernestine and Tommy, resting my chin in my hands, praying he was still alive.

"Psst!" Ernestine nudged me. She made a face and pointed her thumb behind us.

It was Mirabelle's friend Mrs. Mitchell, glaring down at me from a couple of steps up. "Young lady, I'd like to know what happened in that Sunday school class. Ada Jane tells me you're behind this."

"Uh . . . I . . . uh . . ."

"Oh, no. Billie didn't do anything, ma'am," Ernestine said. She hopped up to face Mrs. Mitchell.

I gulped in surprise. Usually, Ernestine hid behind me when we had to answer to a grown-up. She made me do all the talking.

Mrs. Mitchell opened her mouth to say something, but Ernestine cut her off.

"You see . . . uh, well, Mr. Hudson, he . . . uh . . . he forgot the order of the Ten Commandments." Ernestine giggled and batted her eyelashes at Mrs. Mitchell. "So all Billie did was remind him. She's kind of an expert on the commandments."

"That's right," Tommy said. "She even knows them backwards."

"Hmph! That's not the story I heard. I understood that—"

"Clear the way, please!" someone yelled from the church door. Tommy and I jumped up and moved aside as the ambulance men whisked the stretcher back down the steps. I put my hand over my eyes, too scared to look. Suppose Whitey was all covered up with a sheet. That would mean he was dead.

But then I heard a raspy cough. I peeked through my fingers and caught a quick glimpse of Whitey's face. He was blinking in the bright sunlight. I let out a long sigh and leaned against the railing, my legs wobbling with relief.

Once the ambulance and Whitey's family had left for the hospital, Reverend Clarkson canceled church services. "I believe it's only fitting," he told all of us gathered on the sidewalk. "Mirabelle has asked me to join them at the hospital. I'll make calls later today and let everyone know how Whitey is doing."

Ernestine walked the three of us home, and I made plans with her to meet up with Tommy and me at the Main

Street railroad crossing in fifteen minutes, right after we'd changed clothes.

Carla went across the street to play with Tiger. I stood alone on our porch, dreading the thought of facing Daddy Joe. Now that I knew he'd already called the reform school, I didn't trust him one bit.

The empty porch swing creaked in the warm breeze. I stared at it, remembering that hot summer night three years ago when I'd sat there with Daddy and Carla. It'd been late, around eleven. Mama already had fallen asleep, and Daddy had just handed us each our second root beer. "Don't tell your mama," he'd said. "It'll only get her riled up at me again."

"That's because she's afraid Carla will wet the bed," I'd said, feeling the need to stick up for Mama. Besides, Carla slept with me, and I'd been a little worried myself about her getting the second bottle of pop.

"I ain't gonna wet the bed, Daddy," Carla said. She wiped soda off her chin with her pajama sleeve. "Mama don't know nothin'."

I'd raised my eyebrows at Carla, but Daddy had hooted with laughter. "You've got that right, pumpkin," he'd muttered. "Doesn't know a darn thing . . ."

We swung in the dark with our drinks, counting fire-flies and listening to crickets, when Daddy said in a worried voice, "You girls know I love you, don't you?"

I'd looked at him in surprise. Of course I knew he loved us. He'd just given us the second root beer, hadn't he? And we hadn't even had to beg for it. I didn't know one other dad in Myron who would've done that. Not Ernestine's dad, that's for sure. And Tommy's dad, Uncle Warren, he'd probably never given Tommy a root beer in his whole life.

"You know I got laid off from Firestone, right?" Daddy said. He started talking faster then, like he did whenever he argued with Mama. "Well, there's nothing around here that pays any money, so your uncle Gary's been after me to come out to California. He's got me a great job lined up with a construction crew. I'm gonna make big money, girls. Real money, for once. When I get settled, I'm gonna send for you and your mama."

And then I hadn't heard another word he'd said. Because all of a sudden the night had become a big black hole, and it felt like I'd fallen to the very bottom of it.

Daddy swore he'd keep in touch, that he would call long distance and write. "Once a week," he'd told me. "I swear it, baby; I'll write you once a week. All three of you will be out there with me in six months, that's a promise."

His promises never came through. We hadn't made it out to California, and he'd never written once a week like he said, either. I'd gotten a handful of letters the whole time he was gone.

I turned away from the swing, trying to forget the hurt of Daddy leaving. I stuck my head in the door. Good, no one was home. At least I wouldn't have to lie to Mama again. I hurried back to my room to change clothes, but just as I started tying my shoes, the front door opened.

Chapter 27

Daddy Joe's voice filled my room like a blast of freezing air. "Something just came to me," he said. "I think the kids may know where Earl and Warren are hiding. I think they've known all along." I stiffened on the edge of the bed, my fingers frozen to my shoelace.

"Oh, my God!" Mama sounded as though she'd just seen Carla running through the house with scissors. "What makes you say that?"

"It's just a hunch, really, but . . ." Daddy Joe must've walked away, because his voice faded out.

"Good Lord!" Mama said. "If that's true, she could get hurt. I've got to find her."

I leaped off the bed.

"Bud says Earl and Warren will be caught any day," Mama went on. "He says the Indianapolis police think they're on to something. What if Billie gets in the middle of it?"

I flattened my back against the wall, shaking so hard I couldn't catch my breath.

"I'm going across the street to talk to Charlene—to see what she thinks. And I'm calling Bud. I want him to come over here and scare the truth out of Billie. She clams up with me whenever I talk to her about it," Mama said.

I edged to the window. I'd have to make a break for it.

"I have an idea," Daddy Joe said. "You may not like it, but I think we should send the kids . . ."

I strained to hear him, but his voice was too muffled, like he'd walked away again. It didn't matter anyway, because I already knew all about his big idea. He probably had my suitcase packed by the door. I pushed the window screen, watching it fall to the ground.

Daddy Joe's voice rang low and clear down the hallway again. "Whatever you do, don't let her know I told you any of this. She already resents me."

I tried to swing my trembling leg over the windowsill. It might as well have been a tree stump; it wouldn't budge.

"She's going to resent me plenty, too. But I can't have her out all over hell's half acre looking for Earl and Warren. She'll get hurt." Mama's voice grew louder. "I'm checking her room. I want to see if she's hiding anything back here."

I panicked, trying again to heave my leg over the windowsill.

Mama's footsteps creaked up the hallway.

I pictured Daddy Joe revving up the car, a big grin on his face as he prepared to haul me off to the Indianapolis Girls' School. Gathering every bit of strength I had, I forced one leg out the window, then the other. I dropped silently into Mama's azalea bush and took off through the neighbor's backyard, crossing the street and circling in on Tommy's trailer from the back.

I nearly jumped out of my shoes when Carla yelled, "Are you playing hide-and-seek, Billie?" She was hanging upside down from Tommy's tire swing, holding Tiger.

"Where's Tommy?"

"He's inside. I'm baby-sitting the kitty for him." Tiger mewed frantically, trying to claw her way out of Carla's arms.

"She wants to swing faster," Carla said. She spun the tire around again.

I ran to Tommy's bedroom window and rapped on the

screen. "We've got to go. Mama's on her way over here any minute. We're in big trouble. I'll tell you about it later."

I could hardly wait another second to get away, but as soon as Tommy came out the back door, Carla jumped off the tire swing. "Bad kitty! Come back here right now. I ain't done swinging you yet." She ran after the kitten, following it to the tallest tree in Tommy's yard. We watched, helplessly, as Tiger scrambled up the trunk. She didn't stop until she was halfway to the top.

"Shoot! Why'd you let go of her?" Tommy said. "Now I won't be able to get her down. She might fall."

"I didn't let go of her. She jumped away. And look here, she scratched my arm, too." Carla started to bawl. She grabbed her Kimmy doll from the wagon and headed toward the front yard. "I'm going to get Daddy Joe," she called back to us. "He'll get her down. He ain't scared to climb that tree, so there."

"Wait!" I yelled. "Don't —"

She'd already disappeared around the side of the trailer, though. I grabbed Tommy's wrist. "Come on. We can't stay around here; he'll find us."

Tommy wouldn't take his eyes off Tiger. She'd squashed

her belly against the trunk, and her claws were dug into the bark. She twisted her head around and looked down at us, mewing pathetically.

"I can't go anywhere. Look at her. She's crying for me. I've got to help your dad get her down."

"Quit calling him my dad," I snapped. "And come on. Now. We've got to hurry. If he sees me over here, he'll send me back home. You'll get in trouble, too."

"Me? Why? What'd I do?"

"He knows! He knows we've been to where our dads are hiding, and him and Mama are going to tell Bud Castor and your mom. Daddy Joe wants to send us both away to reform school. I heard him."

Tommy's worried gaze darted over his shoulder, then back up the tree at Tiger.

"But what if he can't get her down?"

"He'll figure it out. I've seen him do lots of stuff like that."

He followed me as I raced through the backyard, but he kept looking behind us every couple of seconds, and he wouldn't stop fussing about Tiger. He blamed it all on Carla. "Oh, man. That does it. She ain't ever allowed to touch that cat again, so help me God," he said.

We followed the alley toward the train tracks and met Ernestine by the Main Street crossing. She handed us each a piece of gum and a handful of butterscotch Life Savers as we headed out of town. I wanted her and Tommy to help me make plans about staking out the cabin without getting caught by Old Man Hinshaw, but the only thing either of them talked about was crossing the railroad bridge. I could tell the thought of it scared Tommy to death.

Chapter 28

We followed the tracks out past the glass factory, through the woods, then up the hill and around the big bend to the spot where Tommy had almost gotten hit. He came to a dead stop, pointing it out to Ernestine.

"Oh, man. That's it. That's the place. I almost got killed there." He went into the whole story again, telling her every little detail about the fall, making it sound like he was the one who'd saved me, instead of the other way around.

We inched toward the edge of the bridge, staring down at the Oolitic Reservoir. It looked even bigger than I remembered.

Tommy stood plastered against my back, so close I could feel every steamy puff of his butterscotch breath. I squinted against the sunlight and watched two fat clouds slide across the sky, bump into each other, and change shapes. Trickles of sticky sweat rolled down my cheeks.

"You sure the trains don't run on Sunday?"

I jumped at the sudden squeak of Tommy's voice. He stretched his neck way out, eyeing the water like he'd just seen a crocodile crawl out of it.

"Uh . . . I'm pretty sure it doesn't."

He turned to Ernestine. "Do you remember if it runs on Sunday?"

"Nuh-uh." She chomped furiously on a fresh wad of gum, her gaze fixed on the far side of the bridge.

"Quit worrying about the train. We'll have plenty of time to get off the bridge if we hear it," I said.

Tommy snorted. "Oh, yeah? Well, I almost got killed by the darn thing last time we were out here."

I didn't bother to answer. How many times was he going to remind me about that anyway? I checked behind us again, then took a deep breath before venturing onto the bridge.

"Are you guys coming?" I glanced back at them.

Ernestine's eyes looked glassy, like big green marbles. "Ohmygosh! What if Old Man Hinshaw fires his gun again, like he did at you the last time, Billie?"

"He wasn't shooting at me. He must've been aiming at

a rabbit or something. Besides, he's real old. He probably can't even see us." I sounded way more sure of myself than I felt.

Ernestine took a few shaky steps. She gasped, teetering each way, flapping her arms in frantic circles. "It's making me dizzy."

"It's easier to crawl. Just don't look down," I said.

She dropped stiffly to her hands and knees, following me like a dog—one track at a time—staring straight ahead. "This ain't so bad. You should try crawling," she called to Tommy.

We'd only gone a few feet when I turned back again. Tommy still hadn't budged.

"Quit acting like a scaredy-cat. I'm leaving if you don't come on," I said.

"Shut up! I already told you I'm coming. Just wait a minute."

He moved one foot forward, stopped, then planted the other foot next to it, stopping again. Like baby steps. He never once looked up.

"You're going to get dizzy doing that," I warned him, but he ignored me. I shuffled my feet impatiently. We hadn't even made it over the water yet. At that speed, we'd still be out there the next morning.

"What do you think your dads will do when they see us? You think they'll be surprised?" Ernestine said.

"They'll probably mess their pants," Tommy yelled from behind us.

Ernestine doubled over, holding her stomach as she cackled. She laughed so hard her gum dropped out of her mouth and fell through a slit to the ground.

"And after they mess their pants, they'll tell us to get lost." Tommy took another baby step and stopped again. He was still staring down between the tracks.

"That's not true. Daddy won't tell me to get lost. You're just saying that because you don't want to go. You're too scared to cross the bridge," I said.

He kept his arms plastered against his sides, stiff as stilts. I was several feet ahead of him, but I could still see the fear that flickered across his face.

"I ain't either scared! I don't care, that's all," Tommy said. "I don't care a hoot about my dumb dad."

"How come you don't care about your dad?" Ernestine said. She was still chuckling as she crawled toward me, slow as a snail. Her hair hung in her face.

"Because he's a stupid jerk, that's how come." Tommy's voice cracked. "He doesn't care about me, not one bit. He thinks I'm a sissy. I heard him say it."

Uncle Warren had called Tommy a sissy? Even knowing Uncle Warren, that took me by surprise. I stared at my cousin like I was seeing him for the first time. He looked puny and frail, like a good breeze could send him sailing into the reservoir. I remembered all the years of school, when other kids, big bully kids like Goble, called him a sissy. Even I'd called him names. That was different, though. We were like brother and sister, and he'd called me names, too, like "know-it-all" and "smart aleck." But how would it feel to have your own dad call you a sissy?

No wonder he didn't care what happened to Uncle Warren.

"You ain't a sissy," I said. "You're the one who socked Goble, aren't you? Uncle Warren doesn't know what he's talking about. He's just dumb."

"That's right," Ernestine said. "He's real dumb."

"Maybe I should turn him in. Maybe that's what I should do," Tommy muttered. It looked as if his mind were a million miles away, and in that instant I saw eleven years of hurt, eleven years of wanting the same thing I ached for now—a daddy he didn't have.

"I ain't going," he said, shaking his head. "I'm sorry if I'm a sissy. I'm real sorry." He took a backward step. His arms were still flat to his sides, but he'd started swaying, like he was getting dizzy.

My body tensed. I knew right then we had to get Tommy off the bridge.

"It's okay if you don't go," I said. "I swear it. I don't care. Ernestine can wait by the bridge with you. I'll go by myself."

"That's okay with me," Ernestine said. "I never really wanted to go anyway."

Tommy kept backing up.

"Wait!" I bit my lip, watching as he veered toward the edge of the tracks. "Get on your hands and knees. Crawl like Ernestine."

His face turned gray as ash. He seemed lost, like he didn't hear me. He took another backward step.

"Stop, Tommy! You're too close to the edge!" I cried.

"Don't go any farther," Ernestine said. "You're going to fall."

Tommy kept muttering to himself and moving backward. I started toward him, my arms outstretched, but I couldn't scramble around Ernestine quick enough to grab him.

And then it happened, just like slow motion. Tommy backed up another step. His foot bumped against the rail. He stumbled, flailing his arms as he fell all the way down to the rocky shore of the reservoir.

Ernestine and I screamed—shrill, terrified screams that pierced the thick air. I pulled her up, and we flew back to where the bridge met the land tracks. Tommy lay in a crumpled heap at the bottom of the hill, right by the edge of the water.

"Go back," I begged Ernestine, tugging her arm. "Go back! Hurry! Run back home and get Daddy Joe."

"Do you think he's still—still . . . alive?" Ernestine could hardly talk through her sobs.

"Of course he's alive! He's probably twisted his ankle or something. I'm going after him." I started sliding down the hill, grabbing whatever I could to steady myself.

"Tell Daddy Joe to hurry. But don't tell him where we were going," I hollered.

Ernestine leaped across the railroad tracks like a frightened fawn and disappeared from sight.

"Don't worry, Tommy! I'll be right there," I yelled.

The closer I got, the more I expected him to pop up and yell, "Fooled you!" He didn't, though. He stayed as lifeless as the stones he'd landed on.

I tried hollering to get his attention, but a lump had formed in the back of my throat. Instead, my voice trickled out like a baby's whine. "Stop playing games. Answer me, please. It ain't funny anymore."

All I heard was a family of crows, mocking me from the top of the bridge.

Chapter 29

I skidded the rest of the way down the hill and stumbled over the rocks to Tommy. I hardly recognized him. He was lying on his back, his head turned to the side, his arms spread out like limp, broken wings. His face looked puffy—all purple and bruised. Globs of sticky red blood matted his hair; some of the blood had trickled down the side of his forehead. I slapped my hand over my mouth to keep from screaming when I saw a broken bone sticking out of his lower leg.

"Tommy!" I dropped to the ground and touched his chest lightly. It moved—a slight rise and fall with each breath. I wanted to hold him in my arms, but I was too scared to move him. If only I could get him to open his eyes, to answer me.

Talk to him, something inside my head told me. Keep talking to him. Try to wake him up.

So I told him how Ernestine had run back to town for

Daddy Joe. I told him how it looked like his leg might be broken, but other than that, everything seemed okay. I promised we'd get him to the hospital. Over and over I told Tommy how sorry I was. I told him how I loved him like a brother. I thanked him for sticking by my side for the last two weeks, for not squealing about the money I'd found. "You're the best cousin anyone could ever have," I said.

I made Tommy another promise then. "I'll tell Castor Oil everything. I'll tell him it was me that took the money from the cabin. I'll tell him where I found it, too. You won't be in trouble anymore. I swear it."

Just when I'd about given up hope that he would ever come to, his head moved slightly.

"Open your eyes if you can hear me," I said.

His eyelids fluttered.

"Oh, thank God. Thank God you're alive." I touched his cheek.

He moaned, his eyes opening a bit. "My leg." He muttered so softly I could barely hear him. "My leg hurts."

"Ernestine ran back to get Daddy Joe." I tried to sound normal, to keep the panic out of my voice. "He'll take you to the hospital." I looked up at the tracks. How long had

Ernestine been gone? It seemed like forever. What if she couldn't find Daddy Joe? What if Mama and him had gone for a drive, like they sometimes did on Sundays? And even if Ernestine did find him, it would take a long time before they got back to us—at least half an hour.

Tommy moaned again. The next second his eyes closed. I shook his arm slightly, but he didn't answer. Like a spark, I shot up from the ground.

"I'm going for help right now." My legs quivered; I didn't know if I could even walk, but I couldn't let him die. I had to do something fast. "Listen to me, Tommy. I'm going to find Daddy. He's just over the bridge, so I swear I'll be right back."

I checked one last time to make sure he was still breathing, then started up the hill. I don't know what powered me all the way up it and back over the bridge; it must've been my fear of losing Tommy.

I hurried down the wooded road toward Old Man Hinshaw's cabin. About halfway there, parked between two trees and half buried by overgrowth, was a dark green Studebaker: *Daddy's favorite make of car!* I inched toward the door and peered in the window. Sure enough, I recognized

Daddy's red shirt tossed across the driver's seat. I'd been right, he was at the cabin. Trembling, I backed away from the car and slunk off through the woods, keeping a close eye out for Old Man Hinshaw.

This time the gate to the barbed wire fence hung open. I slipped through it, then hesitated. The thought of going back inside that shack—of actually facing Daddy and Uncle Warren—made my heart drum a wild beat. For more than two weeks now, finding Daddy had been all I could think about. I'd been so worried about him; I'd missed him so much. But now—all of a sudden—I felt scared. My feet didn't want to move.

I couldn't wait any longer, though. I had to get help. I made my way through the high grass and weeds surrounding the cabin, then up the porch steps. When I got to the door, Uncle Warren's voice on the other side of it stopped me cold.

"We'll head over to Illinois on Highway Fifty-four and lay low at Mike's in Decatur. Anybody tries to take us down, I'll take them down first, especially Hinshaw."

I reached for the doorknob.

"I'm going outside," Uncle Warren said. "I need to check—"

He must've turned the handle at the same time I did because the door jerked open, surprising both of us. Uncle Warren stood there without any shirt on, his thick brown hair matted against his head. He scratched his armpit, staring at me. It didn't take but a second before the blank look on his face turned darker than a funnel cloud.

"It's your kid," he said over his shoulder. "What the heck you doing out here?" he snarled to me. "You alone?" His eyes, beady and suspicious, darted toward the fence.

I pushed past him and charged through the door. "Tommy's hurt! Where's Daddy?"

"Hold on there, Billie." Uncle Warren grabbed my arm, pinching it hard. "I asked if you were alone? I'd better get the truth."

"Let go of me!" I yanked away from him and stumbled over a satchel on the floor. When I caught my balance, I looked up and saw Daddy in the kitchen doorway. He had a towel in one hand, a razor in the other. Foamy white shaving cream covered his chin.

I ran to him, throwing my arms around his chest, knocking us both against the wall. The razor flipped out of his hand. "What the—"

"It doesn't matter. It doesn't matter what you've done, Daddy. You've got to come get Tommy. He fell off the railroad bridge. He's hurt bad. His head's all bloody, and there's a bone sticking out of his leg." I buried my face in Daddy's chest, whimpering.

Daddy wiped his chin and tossed the towel toward the kitchen sink. He backed away and pulled my arms from around him. "Who else knows we're here?"

"No one knows. I promise. No one except for Ernestine and Tommy. You've got to help him."

"What the heck's going on?" Uncle Warren snarled from the other side of the room. He cupped his hand over a cigarette and lit it. "What the heck you talking about? Tommy's hurt? What is this—some kind of trick?"

I glared at him. Why didn't he believe me? Didn't he care about Tommy at all? Mama always said everyone had a heart in there somewhere, except some were way smaller than others. But Uncle Warren? His heart had shrunk into a tiny ice pellet. You'd need a microscope to find it.

I turned back to Daddy, pulling his hand, pleading with him. "It ain't a trick, I swear. Please!"

His eyes flicked to Uncle Warren, and a heavy silence

crept into the room, muffling everything but the sound of my heart thumping. Daddy ran his hands through his wet hair and started talking fast.

"Baby, we ain't got time for jokes. You know we're in some trouble here, don't you?"

I swallowed a hiccup. "But this ain't any—"

"Lookit, baby." He dug his hand down his pocket, rattling stuff around and pulling out a thick wad of bills. "Here. Take that. Run on back home now, and buy you and your sister something pretty. Get that bicycle you want. But you got to promise me something. You got to promise you won't tell anyone you saw us out here."

I stared at the crumpled money in my hand.

"You swear, baby? You swear you won't tell anyone?"

I barely nodded. I couldn't take my eyes off the money.

Daddy must've thought I wanted more, because he yanked another handful of bills from his pocket. "Here. Give some of this to your mama." He started jabbering so fast I could hardly understand him. "Listen here, baby. This ain't a game. Warren and me got to go. I want you to run on home. I don't want any bad stuff going down with you out here."

I shook my head, angry tears filling my eyes. I pushed his hand away.

"I'm not joking. Tommy's hurt bad. Ernestine went to town after Daddy Joe, but they ain't back yet."

"You say Joe Hughes is on the way?" Uncle Warren shot across the room, sticking his face up against mine. "I thought you said no one else knew we were out here." He nodded toward the door and snapped at Daddy. "Get everything in the car. Now. We got trouble coming."

"But what about Tommy?" I cried. "You can't leave him!"

"Baby, there's nothing we can do for Tommy," Daddy said. "It's best to let Joe take care of him."

Uncle Warren pulled on a T-shirt and started throwing stuff in his satchel. "That's right. Hughes will take care of him. Besides, the boy can't be hurt that bad, if he's conscious and he's sending you after help. Sounds to me like another one of his stunts." He flicked his cigarette outside the door, turning back to Daddy with a sour look on his face. "You need to get rid of something this red-hot minute, if you know what's good for us."

Daddy jiggled a set of car keys in his pocket. His eyes

flitted around the room, then caught mine for one split second, just long enough for me to see the stranger he'd become.

It was then I got it. It was then I understood that getting away with the money meant more to Daddy than anything. Even me.

"Tommy's going to be all right, baby. Joe will take better care of him than we could. You got to go now. Give me a big hug, you hear?" Daddy walked toward me, his arms outstretched.

I threw the money down and backed toward the door. "You're just like him," I said, pointing to Uncle Warren. "You don't care one bit about me or Tommy."

"Baby, don't talk like that," Daddy called after me as I ran outside. "You know I love you."

"I ain't your stupid baby."

"Hey! Keep your mouth shut about what you saw out here," Uncle Warren yelled. "And tell Tommy I said to stay the hell off that railroad bridge."

"Shut up, creep! I hate you. I hate both of you." Blinded by tears, I ran, tripping over Old Man Hinshaw's No Trespassing sign. I scrambled to my feet, yanked the sign out of the ground, and hurled it toward the shack.

I took off again, away from Daddy's shouts about how sorry he was. Once I made it out the gate, I raced through the woods back toward the bridge.

When I reached Daddy's car, a noise in the woods startled me. And then I saw him, Old Man Hinshaw. He had his shotgun, and he was headed my way.

Chapter 30

I crouched against the Studebaker, grabbing the fender to steady myself. If Old Man Hinshaw came near the car, he'd see me for sure. Ever so slowly I craned my neck around the taillight, watching him.

He stopped.

I froze. What was he doing?

He stood straight up, his head cocked to one side. I didn't dare move. If I made even the slightest sound, he'd hear it.

Then just as suddenly as he'd stopped, Old Man Hinshaw darted back through the woods. He was headed toward the cabin. Was he planning to slip up on Daddy and Uncle Warren? Maybe I should go back and warn them. I could probably beat him there. But what about Tommy? I couldn't forget the sight of his bruised, bloody face, of that broken bone in his leg. He needed me.

Without giving it another thought, I turned toward the

railroad bridge. Daddy and Uncle Warren would have to face Old Man Hinshaw by themselves.

By the time I made it across the reservoir thick clouds covered the sun, making the air feel like a steam bath. Ernestine and Daddy Joe weren't anywhere in sight, but I could see Tommy from the tracks, still lying where I'd left him. Once more I skidded down the rocky hill, preparing myself for the worst.

My heart pounded with joy when I saw his open eyes. I dropped beside him, feeling his forehead.

"What happened?" His murmur sounded pinched with pain.

"I went to Old Man Hinshaw's cabin, but I couldn't find anyone. We'll have to wait for Ernestine and Daddy Joe to get back. How's your head?"

"It hurts. But not as bad as my leg."

I checked his broken bone again; nothing had changed. "It doesn't look that bad," I lied. "Just a little swollen. Make sure you don't move it, though."

"What happened?" Tommy's voice was so groggy I could hardly understand him. "I can't see so good. Where are we?"

"Don't you remember? You fell off the railroad bridge."

"What railroad bridge?"

I wiped the sweat from my brow, trembling. How come he kept asking me these questions? Had something happened to his brain? I peered into his eyes. They looked dazed, distant.

"Billie!" Daddy Joe's deep voice echoed through the reservoir. A flood of relief washed over me when I saw him standing at the top of the hill.

I waved my arms over my head. "Down here! Hurry! Tommy's hurt. His leg's broken."

"Hold tight," Daddy Joe called. "I'll be right there." Instead of starting down the hill, though, he disappeared. After a minute or so of waiting I jumped up, pacing back and forth next to Tommy, kicking at the stones around my feet.

Daddy Joe reappeared, holding two bushy tree limbs. He clutched them under one arm and scaled down the rocks like a mountain climber. It didn't seem like any time before he was on the ground beside me, checking Tommy's pulse.

"Has he been moved at all?"

"No." I shook my head, feeling panic well up in me again. Had I done something wrong? Maybe I should've turned Tommy on his side to help him breathe better. "I didn't think I was supposed to move him."

"You thought right," Daddy Joe said with a quick nod. "Good job. Now tell me what happened."

In a shaky voice I described how Tommy had backed up on the bridge and tripped over the rail. As I told the story, the picture of Tommy's terrified face at the moment he fell kept swirling around my head, and it was all I could do to keep talking. I took a deep breath, then went on to explain how I'd climbed down the hill to help him while Ernestine had run back to town. I stopped before getting to the part about why we'd been crossing the bridge in the first place. And I didn't say a word about how I'd found Daddy and Uncle Warren at Old Man Hinshaw's cabin. I couldn't stand for Tommy to hear that his own dad wouldn't come back to help him.

Daddy Joe listened, answering me with quick nods and uh-huhs while he tended to Tommy. He checked every inch of the broken leg like he was a real doctor. He listened to Tommy's lungs, looked in his eyes, and inspected his neck and head. He even had him wriggle his toes and fingers. "I need to make sure there's not a back injury," he said.

But when Daddy Joe started asking him questions about the fall, you would've thought Tommy didn't have a brain left in his head, some of the silly answers he gave.

"How come he's acting so goofy? Do you think his brain got knocked loose or something?" I whispered.

"His brain's just fine. He has a concussion, that's all. It's normal for him to act a little hazy. He may never remember exactly what happened out here today." Daddy Joe dabbed at the blood around Tommy's eye. "Don't you worry about a thing, kiddo. We'll get you all fixed up."

Kiddo? I jerked my head back in surprise. I never knew Daddy Joe said stuff like that; at least he never had to me. He'd never called me anything but my name, and half the time it sounded like it pained him to say it.

Tommy opened his eyes and managed a weak grin,

and for the first time since he'd fallen I felt like he might be okay.

Daddy Joe had me pull the leaves and small twigs off the tree branches he'd brought down the hill, explaining how he was going to make a splint for the broken leg.

"It's an open fracture. We need to stabilize it before I can get him up the hill."

"You mean we're going to carry him?"

"That's the plan." He glanced around the deserted reservoir. "It doesn't look like we're getting airlifted out of here anytime soon." He gave me a determined smile, then got to work preparing the splint. He snapped a tree limb in two, showing me how the leafy twigs would pad the splint. He used his pocketknife to cut a couple of long, skinny twigs from the limb. "These are flexible but strong," he said. "We'll use them to hold the splint in place."

Tommy barely uttered a word the whole time Daddy Joe worked on his leg. I held his hand, my own face stinging whenever he cried in pain. I prayed his fuzzy memory would make him forget this had happened because of me. So far the only thing he'd managed to talk about was Tiger.

"Did you get her out of the tree?" he asked.

Daddy Joe nodded. "Took a while, though. That's one feisty kitten you got there. Reminds me of a certain cousin of yours."

I saw the twinkle in Daddy Joe's eyes, but I didn't smile back. I still wasn't sure I could trust him. What was he really thinking about me behind that twinkle, that I was a thief who needed to go to reform school?

I watched in silence as he finished Tommy's splint. I couldn't get over how much he knew about first aid. I'd never figured him to be that smart.

"Did you learn all that in the army?"

"Yep. In Korea." He tested Tommy's toes to make sure they hadn't gone numb. "I learned a lot over there as a medic, bandaged all kinds of wounds." He sat back for a moment, looking at me. "Guess the only thing I didn't learn was how to mend a wounded heart. I'm real sorry about that, Billie."

I wanted to answer him, but my guilty conscience stopped me. Would he still be sorry if he found out Tommy's broken leg and concussion were my fault? Would he still want to be my stepdad, or would he want to get rid of me, like Ada Jane said? I stared into the reservoir, watching the water ripple. I didn't know what to think anymore.

Once the splint was in place, Daddy Joe picked Tommy up like he was a delicate piece of china.

"Where's Ernestine?" I asked him. "How'd she find you so quick?"

"She found me near the glass factory. I was already headed this way, looking for you."

"But how'd you know where we'd gone?"

"You can thank your little sister for that. She overheard you talking about crossing the railroad bridge."

I gulped. I was in for it now. Mama for sure would hang me out to dry. But Daddy Joe didn't even sound mad. He told me he'd sent Ernestine back home to have Mama call an ambulance.

"We'd better hurry so I can meet up with it," he said, starting up the hill.

I crawled after him, watching as he took the slope in huge strides. Even with Tommy cradled in his arms, Daddy Joe made it up the rocks in less time than it took me to brush my teeth. He stopped at the top and waited for me. I was almost there when the small shrub I pulled on came uprooted. I cried out, grabbing at a cluster of loose stones. In a flash, Daddy Joe leaned over and took my arm. He whisked me up next to him. "Can't have two of you with broken legs, now can I?"

"Thanks." I brushed my knees off and glanced at him, feeling a little shy. "Um . . . how are we going to find the ambulance? There aren't any roads that come back here."

"I'm taking Tommy over the bridge. There's a lane that runs through the woods out to the road by Fred Hinshaw's house. I'm meeting the ambulance there."

Over the bridge? By Old Man Hinshaw's?

My heart started to race.

"I want you to turn back now, Billie. I don't like the idea of you crossing this bridge. It's bad enough I have to risk it with Tommy," he said.

No! I couldn't let them go without me. Nobody but me knew what might be waiting on the other side of the bridge. What if they ran into Daddy and Uncle Warren? Or even worse, what if Old Man Hinshaw came after them with his shotgun? I sped to the bridge ahead of Daddy Joe, before he could stop me.

"I'm going," I yelled over my shoulder. "I promised Tommy I'd stick with him. Besides, I'm not scared of crossing the bridge."

"Be careful then. And don't look down. You might get dizzy."

I waved to let him know I'd heard him. I wondered what he'd think if he knew I'd already crossed that bridge so many times I could've done it with my eyes closed.

I hurried across, waiting for them on the other side. It wrenched my heart to see Tommy hanging on to Daddy Joe, looking so scared and helpless. As soon as they caught up to me, we headed in the direction of the highway. I followed Daddy Joe up the lane, thinking I'd better warn him how Old Man Hinshaw patrolled the woods with a shotgun. But a gunshot stopped me cold.

Daddy Joe grabbed my arm. "There must be a hunter out here. Stay beside me."

Then came the second shot. It sounded closer. Fear crept over my body like a spider's thick web.

"Stop shooting!" Daddy Joe's voice boomed through the woods. "I've got kids with me!"

"It's not a hunter," I said. "It's Old Man Hinshaw or maybe Uncle War—"

A horn blared.

The green Studebaker came barreling up the narrow lane, straight at us.

Chapter 31

I couldn't even scream. I stood rooted to the ground as the Studebaker sped toward us. Daddy was driving. Uncle Warren hung out the window on the passenger's side with a long rifle aimed at something behind the car.

"Get down, Billie!" Daddy Joe reached out and yanked me around the rough bark of a tree trunk. I fell against him, knocking into Tommy. He yelped with pain.

"What's wrong?" he whimpered. "What's wrong with my leg?"

Daddy Joe clutched Tommy to his chest with one arm, trying to calm him down. He held me flat against the tree with his other arm. I clung to his shirt sleeve when a third shot rang out from somewhere in the woods.

"Don't shoot!" I heard Daddy holler to Uncle Warren from inside the car. "You might hit the kids!"

"I'd like to get my hands on that crazy old son of a—"

And then the Studebaker tore away, spitting chunks of dirt out from under its tires.

Daddy Joe wiped Tommy's sweaty cheek. He shifted him in his arms to keep the bad leg from getting knocked around. "Hang in there, son. We're going to get you help just as soon as possible." He peered around the tree, then back at me, his face drawn and serious. "I need the truth, Billie. What's going on out here?"

I stood trembling against the trunk, my ears still ringing from the shotgun blast.

"It's Old Man Hinshaw. That was him shooting at the car." I told Daddy Joe the whole story then—as much of it as I could, anyway, even if it meant I'd for sure end up in reform school. I told him how Uncle Warren and Daddy had been hiding in the cabin and how I'd seen Old Man Hinshaw headed that way with his gun.

The creases in his forehead deepened. "Listen carefully. Fred Hinshaw is not to be messed with; he's unstable. We're going out to the highway now, as fast as we can. I want you to stay in front of me, where I can see you."

I nodded and took off ahead of him. After we'd walked just a short distance, Tommy started crying again, and

Daddy Joe stopped to soothe him. I'd already gotten several feet ahead of them when I heard some leaves rustle next to me. I hesitated for a moment, thinking it must be a possum. I glanced into the bushes. A long, skinny arm whipped out from the leaves and wrapped around my neck, squeezing the breath out of me.

Old Man Hinshaw yanked me behind the bush. His hot whiskey breath skipped across the back of my neck. "You out here trespassin' on my property again, girl? You after somethin' of mine? Fred Hinshaw ain't takin' to that. Oh, no, he ain't."

I gasped for air, croaking, "Let go!" I must've startled him, because his grip loosened. I lurched forward, falling to the ground. When I rolled over, I was looking straight into his wild, bloodshot eyes.

"I'm not after anything! I swear it—"

"Put the gun down, Fred." Daddy Joe moved toward us slowly, not taking his eyes off Old Man Hinshaw. "Leave her be. I'll give you whatever it is you want."

Old Man Hinshaw raised his gun at Daddy Joe. "I'll whip the snot out of this here young'un; she's a trespasser, deserves a good whippin'. Tried to pull a fast one on me, but

I ain't senile yet. Fred Hinshaw still knows a thing or two about a thing or two."

"You're right, Fred." Daddy Joe took a step closer. He didn't sound scared of Old Man Hinshaw at all. In fact, you would've thought they were passing time on a street corner the way Daddy Joe buddied up to him. "My girl didn't have any business out here, messing on your property. Her mom and I will tend to that soon enough. And I'll give you whatever we owe you, soon as I can get to my wallet."

He kept talking, his voice sounding calm and matter-of-fact. "I've got a hurt boy here, Fred. He fell off the bridge; you can see for yourself."

Old Man Hinshaw looked at Tommy, who stared back at him with big, frightened eyes. "Shouldn't of been out on that durn bridge, boy," he said.

"I'd like for you to help us out, Fred," Daddy Joe said. "We need to get him to the hospital."

"Ain't no hospital out here."

"Can't argue with that," Daddy Joe said. "That's why we're looking for the highway. I hear you know these woods like the back of your hand. Thought you might oblige me by showing us the way. I'd be mighty appreciative."

Old Man Hinshaw lowered his gun, staring off through the trees like he might be thinking things over. He wiped his forehead with the crusted sleeve of his shirt. "The highway's down this here dirt road. Follow me." Then he turned back to me and said, "Close your mouth and git up, girl. We ain't got all day."

Daddy Joe and I followed him along the lane, the heavy silence of the woods broken only by our footsteps and Tommy's whimpering. Every once in a while he muttered something about Tiger or his bicycle, but none of what he said made any sense—it sounded like gibberish. It still scared me to hear him ramble like that. Daddy Joe didn't seem worried. He patted Tommy's arm and answered him like everything was going to be okay.

I heard the sirens as soon as we made it to the clearing that led out to the highway.

"What's that?" Tommy said. "Are they coming for me?"

Old Man Hinshaw's head perked up. He stopped, one hand flat to his side, the other cupped to his ear. He motioned us ahead of him, and the gun came back up. "Go on. Go on, now. Git! I ain't inclined to meet up with no city officials today."

I edged around him, staring at his gun barrel the whole time. He backed away and faded into the thick shelter of the woods.

The ambulance turned onto our lane from the highway. I stopped dead in my tracks when I saw the flashing lights of Bud Castor's police car following it. The closer they got, the more confused and scared I felt. Daddy Joe for sure would tell Bud what had happened in the woods, and once the truth came out, how could I face everyone? I'd have to rat on my own daddy. I'd have to admit what he'd done.

I knew what highway him and Uncle Warren planned on taking. I even knew where they were going. But now I felt scared. Could I really send my own daddy to prison?

Daddy Joe must've been reading my mind. "Billie, I want to tell you something," he said. His deep voice startled me, but this time it didn't make me mad. It didn't make me turn away. This time I listened.

"I'm going to have to tell the police what I saw. It's my responsibility. But whatever else happened between you and your daddy out here today—whatever else you might know—is your story to tell, not mine. You're a brave young girl; I know you'll do the right thing." He put his arm around my shoulder. I hesitated for a moment, then leaned my head against his side.

"I want you to know that no matter what you do, no matter what you say, I'm here for you," he said.

I looked in his eyes, but I didn't have a chance to answer him. The doors to the ambulance and Bud's police car flew open, and the very next second I was swept into Mama's arms.

Chapter 32

I stood next to Mama as the ambulance pulled away with Tommy and Aunt Charlene. I couldn't quit thinking how it was my fault, how I'd talked Tommy into coming with me in the first place, then called him a chicken for not wanting to cross the bridge.

I climbed into the backseat of Bud's car next to Mama. Carla had already snuggled beside Daddy Joe in the front seat, humming and chattering away to her Kimmy doll. For some reason, the sight of her sitting next to him, so carefree, made me even sadder.

Ernestine slid in beside me and shut the door. Once we got settled in the car, she nudged me and pointed to Bud in the front seat, whispering, "I didn't say anything about you-know-what to you-know-who."

Castor Oil took off his sunglasses and looked at us through the rearview mirror. His eyes were lit up with curiosity.

"Now here's what I'd like to know," he said. He adjusted his mirror to get a better view of us. "Just what were you kids doing out there on that bridge? Were you looking for someone?"

An uneasy silence filled the car. Ernestine nudged me again.

"That's exactly what I want to know," Mama said. "I'm sure Ernestine's parents will want an answer, too, as soon as they hear what's happened."

Ernestine clamped her teeth over her lip like she'd been sucking on a lemon. Neither of us said a word. I felt bad for Ernestine. I didn't want her to get in trouble; she hadn't asked for any of this. Neither had Tommy. They'd only gone along to make me feel better. I thought about what good friends they'd been. Tommy hadn't ever ratted on me after I'd found the money, and Ernestine chose me over Ada Jane. And what about the promise I'd made Tommy, that I'd tell Bud Castor the truth?

I squirmed around in the seat, trying to sink out of Bud's view. By now the secrets I carried felt heavier than a suitcase full of bricks. From the corner of my eye I looked at Mama. Her face was lined with worry and unanswered questions. Didn't she deserve the truth, even if I was too chicken to tell her?

Chicken.

I cringed at the word. That's what I'd been calling Tommy the last two weeks, every time he didn't want to go along with me. A chicken.

But who was the chicken now?

I swallowed a gulp of air, praying Mama would forgive me. I took her hand. "Uh . . . there's something I'd better tell you before we get to the hospital. . . ."

After I finished talking, after I told them everything, Mama held me so tight I thought she would crush my ribs. She had a few choice words to say about Daddy, and Uncle Warren, too—words that made Carla giggle into her Kimmy doll.

Castor Oil turned on his siren. "We're on official police business now," he said. He sped down the highway at least eighty miles an hour toward the hospital. Once we got there, he let us run in to ask about Tommy while he called the Millerstown police. The next thing I knew we were surrounded by cops in the hospital waiting room.

Ernestine sat next to me, between Mama and Daddy Joe. She held my hand as I told my story again. I told about finding the money at Old Man Hinshaw's shack, about Daddy's smudged note I still had hidden in my closet, and about what'd happened after Tommy fell off the bridge. Castor Oil kept interrupting every few seconds, nodding and saying things like "Uh-huh" and "Those were my suspicions all along."

Finally, with tears burning my eyes, I told the police the description of the Studebaker and what highway Daddy and Uncle Warren planned on taking. "They're supposed to stop in Decatur at Uncle Mike's to lay low and maybe change cars," I said.

I felt so rotten afterward, especially when I remembered how I'd promised Daddy I wouldn't squeal. Would he ever forgive me? I worried all night about him, praying him and Uncle Warren wouldn't do anything crazy when the cops came after them.

Ernestine sat waiting on the bench outside Fuzzy's Tavern the next day as I walked up with Mama, Daddy Joe, and Carla. I couldn't wait to talk to her. We'd just left Bud Castor's police station, where we'd learned Daddy and Uncle Warren had been caught the day before, only a couple of hours after I'd told on them.

"You did the right thing by telling, Billie. I'm proud of you," Mama said. She gave me a hug before going inside the diner to start a batch of french fries for her Monday lunch customers.

Ernestine handed me some Milk Duds. "What's going on?" she asked.

"They caught Daddy and Uncle Warren."

She blinked her big green eyes and stuffed candy in her mouth. "For real?"

"Yeah. They found them somewhere by Illinois. They're in jail already." I sat down next to her, wishing I felt as proud of myself as Mama did about me. I couldn't get over the feeling of being a traitor—no better than Benedict Arnold. I thought about Daddy being dragged into Pendleton and shoved into a cell. They'd probably make him wear one of those black-and-white striped prison suits, like the ones the convicts on television wore. I wondered what he'd be eating for lunch. I doubted it would be french fries and hamburgers, like I'd be having.

More like bread and water. That's what I heard they got for almost every meal at the Pendleton Penitentiary.

Fuzzy Hilton was leaning against the door of his tavern, chewing tobacco. He spit a wad out toward the street and asked Daddy Joe, "You seen the boy yet?"

"That's where Billie and I are headed, soon as I get the car."

"You tell him Fuzzy says to stay off them railroad bridges."

"Will do." Daddy Joe took off down the street, waving at us. "I'll pick you up here in a few minutes, Billie."

After he left, Carla came out of the diner with her Kimmy doll. She danced the doll on the bench beside me, singing a rhyme to herself, the same rhyme I'd sang hundreds of times with Ernestine and Tommy, way back when we were in kindergarten:

Ho, ho, ho and a bottle of rum,
Pendleton ain't too much fun.
You'd better watch your P's and Q's,
Or Pendleton's the place for you.
Ho, ho, ho and a bottle of ale.
Pendleton's a bad ol' jail,
If you don't—

"Hush," I said, before she could finish the second verse. "That song ain't nice to sing."

Carla stuck her lower lip out, and her thumb started working its way to her mouth. "I can sing it if I want to, can't I, Ernestine?"

"You shouldn't, really," Ernestine said. "It might make Billie feel bad."

"Do you feel still bad, Billie?" Carla asked. "Like last night when you cried."

"Kind of," I muttered.

Carla handed Ernestine her doll and climbed on my lap, taking my chin in her sticky hands. "Don't feel sad," she said. "I won't sing that song no more, I swear it. And Mama said our real Daddy's gonna be okay. She promised me so."

"That's right. He'll probably be out of Pendleton in no time," Ernestine said, but I knew she was just trying to make me feel better.

"I bet he'll be out of jail before Ada Jane is," Carla said. "Won't he, Billie?"

Ernestine took my arm. "What? What happened to Ada Jane?"

"She got took to Pendleton, too," Carla said.

"She did not," I said. "You shouldn't go spreading things that aren't true."

"Did her parents find the money?" Ernestine asked.

I nodded. "She's in big trouble. I told on her. Castor Oil went over there last night, and she finally told the truth. They found the church money under her bed. She said she was going to give it back."

"Yeah, right," Ernestine said. "Maybe after she bought five more hula hoops and a thousand root beer floats." A giggle popped out of my mouth, and Ernestine snorted, and then we fell against each other laughing. Even Carla joined in, except I'm not sure she was clear about the joke of it.

As I sat on Fuzzy's bench, I thought how good it felt to be with my best friend again. To be sitting side by side, joking and laughing, without the cloud of the stolen church money or Ada Jane hovering over us. "You think your mom will let you hang out with me again?" I asked. "You know, after she finds out I didn't steal anything."

"Yeah, I'm sure she will. I heard her tell my dad she misses you. And Ada Jane was starting to get on their nerves. My dad said she whines too darn much."

Ernestine dug around in her pocket but came up empty-handed. I knew what she was after so I reached in my own pocket and pulled out three pieces of Bazooka. I'd found them on the floor of our bedroom closet that morning. I gave one to Ernestine, one to Carla, and unwrapped the other for myself. Then I thought about Tommy, and the gum didn't taste nearly as sweet as usual. I wondered how long it'd be before he got out of the hospital.

Ernestine stretched her gum out of her mouth and twirled it around her finger. Carla copied her.

"What did they say about you going on the bridge?" I asked. "Are you in trouble?" I was nervous to hear the answer but felt like I had to know. After all, I'd been the one who'd begged her to go along with me.

"Can't ride my bike for two weeks."

"I'm sorry." I couldn't bring myself to look at her, knowing how much she loved that bike and how it was my fault she couldn't ride it. I picked up a pebble and scratched a heart on the sidewalk, then wrote "E & B" in the middle of it.

"That's okay; I don't care," Ernestine said. She took the

pebble and wrote "best friends 4 ever" under our initials. "Ada Jane messed the handlebars up anyway. What about you? Are you in trouble?"

"Yes, she sure is," Carla said. "Mama says Billie can't go nowhere but the diner for two whole weeks."

"My mom says she's going to see your mom today. Maybe she'll talk her into letting you come to the diner for floats. I'll make them for free," I said. I put an exclamation point after "4 ever," then nudged Ernestine in the side until she giggled.

A few minutes later Daddy Joe pulled up in the station wagon. When I opened the door, I noticed a box in the backseat. "What's that?" A frightened mew answered me, and I looked over the seat to see Tiger scratching at the side of the box.

"Are we taking her to see Tommy? Will they let her in the hospital?"

"Yes and no," Daddy Joe answered. "I've got big pockets."

I giggled, reaching into the box for Tiger. She clung to my blouse with her tiny, sharp claws as we headed out of town. Once we got to the highway I rolled my window down, letting the wind whip my hair into tangles.

I couldn't quit thinking about Daddy, though. The picture of him being locked up in Pendleton kept crawling across my mind, over and over. I held tight to Tiger and stuck my head out the window, wishing the wind could blow all my worries down the highway.

Chapter 33

I sunk back in the car seat with my eyes closed. I didn't know what to expect when we got to the hospital. Suppose Tommy had gotten worse during the night and no one had told us? I worried about Aunt Charlene, too. Would she be mad at me about the accident? She'd spent the night at the hospital, and I hadn't seen her since yesterday.

We drove through Millerstown and passed by the Henderson County Bank that Daddy robbed. I watched as a group of people walked inside. One of the women was carrying a little girl with a doll in her arms. She reminded me of Carla, kind of silly acting. All of a sudden the scariness of what Daddy and Uncle Warren had done hit me like a slap across the cheek. What if that little girl had been in the bank the day they robbed it?

I thought about how Daddy and Uncle Warren had threatened people, how they'd stolen all that money— thousands of dollars. What if they'd gone free and tried to rob another bank, only this time someone got hurt, some little kid like Carla?

I stared out the window, scratching Tiger's ears as she purred in my arms, thinking about how Daddy's actions had hurt so many people. For the last three years I'd never accepted what Mama had said about him. All I knew was that I'd missed him, so bad I couldn't think straight. I missed his handsome face and his quick grin. I missed the way he kidded around with me and how he always made me laugh.

I remembered all the times she'd said Daddy had never grown up. It'd made me mad before, but now I kind of understood what Mama meant. And I finally believed her that he got fired from the Firestone plant because he stole from them, just like he'd taken the sparklers and the pie and the bank money.

I knew now I'd done the right thing by telling the police. Daddy had to face up to his crime, and at least I'd stopped him and Uncle Warren from doing something worse. I took a deep breath, letting my guilt evaporate into the steamy summer air.

I glanced at Daddy Joe. He was whistling Elvis Presley's

song "You Ain't Nothing but a Hound Dog" while he tapped on the steering wheel. I straightened up, eyeing him with surprise. I never knew he could whistle. I never even knew he liked Elvis Presley. I watched him—real curious—realizing how much stuff I didn't know about him, like what flavor ice cream he liked best, or why he never went to church on Sunday. He wasn't anything like my real daddy; that much I knew. He didn't tell racy jokes or twirl Carla so fast on the swing she couldn't catch her breath. Daddy Joe didn't do magic tricks, or secretly tie my shoelaces together, or swig milk out of the container behind Mama's back.

I realized other things Daddy Joe had never done, either, things that made me feel bad about the way I'd treated him. He never forgot to make lunch for Carla and me—even if it wasn't all that good, and he never complained he was too tired to go to work.

Daddy Joe did quiet things, important things, like fixing our broken bicycles and helping Carla collect old Popsicle sticks. He made sure we brushed our teeth and drank all our milk at breakfast. And one thing I knew for sure: He wouldn't be going to jail anytime soon, leaving me and Mama and Carla behind with a sorry mess to clean up.

I was thinking about all this when I realized we'd already pulled into the hospital parking lot. I looked up at the big building, and my heart skipped a beat. What if Tommy had gone into a coma? Or what if he was wide awake and curious, wanting to know why his dad hadn't come to help him yesterday? What would I tell him?

Daddy Joe stood outside the car, waiting for me, but I couldn't make myself touch the door handle. I pictured Tommy's curious face, quizzing me about what had happened at the cabin, and I didn't think I could stand to answer him.

Daddy Joe opened the door and knelt beside me. He tickled Tiger's chin. "Is something on your mind, Billie?"

I swallowed the lump in my throat, struggling to hold everything in. I didn't want to think about it anymore. I didn't want to cry. All of a sudden, though, the plug popped. Everything spilled out—all of my hurt, my anger at Daddy, my fears for Tommy. I started to sob, big gulping sobs that doubled me over. I buried my face in Tiger's fur.

"There now," Daddy Joe said, patting my shoulder. "Let it all out, kiddo. You must be hurting pretty bad."

I sniffled, looking at him through my tears. I remembered what Ada Jane had said and what I thought I'd heard him say. "Are you really going to send me to reform school?"

"Reform school?" he said, looking surprised. "Now where'd you get an idea like that?"

"Ada Jane said you'd already called the school."

"What?" His eyes widened. He shook his head slowly before saying, "You know Ada Jane pretty well. What are the odds of her telling the truth?"

"Not much."

"Exactly." He took my hands, looking straight into my eyes. "Listen to me, Billie. I would never—*ever*—in a thousand years even consider sending one of my kids to reform school." He pushed a strand of hair off my forehead, like Mama always did. "You believe me?"

I nodded.

"Okay. Now that we've got that straight, are you ready to see your cousin?"

"Yep."

"While you're visiting with Tommy, I'll run in and check on Whitey."

Whitey! I stopped in my tracks. I'd forgotten all about him being in the hospital, too.

"We heard from Mirabelle that he's doing much better today." Daddy Joe pushed the door to the lobby open, but I couldn't force myself to walk inside.

"Uh . . ." I backed away from the door, my heart tap-dancing against my ribs. I had to explain what'd happened at church—to give him my side of the story—before Mirabelle had a chance to turn him against me.

Daddy Joe stood with his back to the door, watching me curiously.

"I didn't mean it!" I blurted out. "I didn't mean to cause Whitey's heart attack." Barely stopping for a breath, I told him everything that happened at Sunday School the day before, even the part about Whitey and the commandments.

He listened to my story without saying a word, without moving a muscle in his face. When I got to the part about correcting Whitey over "Thou Shalt Not Steal" being the eighth commandment, a twinkle danced across his dark eyes. "So that's what happened?" he said when I finished.

I toed the ground. "Yes. I'm really sorry for causing Whitey's attack."

"Let's get something straight here, Billie."

I could hardly bring myself to look at him.

"You did not cause Whitey's heart problem. Or his asthma."

"I didn't?"

"No. Far from it. Whitey's had asthma ever since I can remember. And his heart? Well, let's just say he doesn't take very good care of himself. It has nothing to do with you. Trust me on that. Okay, kiddo?"

"Okay."

We walked to the far end of the hospital lobby, where Daddy Joe stopped at the information desk and asked for Whitey's room number.

"Are you family?" The lady at the desk looked at us over the top of her glasses.

Daddy Joe nodded. I bit back a laugh when he shoved Tiger's mewing mouth into his pants pocket.

"Room one-oh-four," she said, looking at us suspiciously. "Don't stay longer than ten minutes."

"You want to come in here with me before we visit Tommy?" Daddy Joe asked outside Whitey's room.

"Uh . . . I . . ."

"It's okay, Billie. It might make you feel better to see he's doing well."

"Okay." I hesitated before peering inside the room. Whitey was sitting up in the bed, propped into place by about a hundred pillows. His lunch of applesauce, mashed potatoes, and meat loaf sat on a tray in front of him, and Mirabelle had a spoon headed straight to his mouth.

"I ain't going nowhere until this lunch is ate up," she said. "I know it ain't home cooking, but you got to get your nourishment. Them's the exact words of your doctor: 'get your nourishment.'"

From behind me, Daddy Joe coughed softly. Mirabelle's face crinkled into a smile at the sight of him.

"Well, lordy be! Lookit what the cat drug in, Whitey."

"Guess you could say so." Daddy Joe chuckled. He pulled Tiger out of his pocket and held her up for Mirabelle to see. "Billie and I and this little kitten stopped in to see how Uncle Whitey is doing."

"I've been better," Whitey croaked. He patted his chest. "It was a close call. Yes-sir-ee. I thought the Lord was calling me up."

"He'll call you up over my dead body!" Mirabelle said

in a huff. She wiped a glob of potatoes from his chin and turned back to Daddy Joe. "He ain't doing too bad, considering all the hullabaloo he's been through over the last few weeks. The doctors say his heart will be okay, say it was mostly the asthma. Main thing is them nervous attacks he gets. Just works hisself up over certain things too much." She looked straight at me.

I took a couple of steps toward the bed. Mirabelle watched every move I made like I was a panther, getting ready to pounce on Whitey.

Daddy Joe started teasing with her then, getting her to pet the kitten and tell him how terrible the hospital food was. I edged over to Whitey's bedside. He looked as pale as the sheets tucked around him.

"I'm real sorry about your attack yesterday, Whitey. I shouldn't ever have said that stuff."

To my surprise, Whitey patted my hand and said, "None of this here is your fault. I just got me a wore-out old ticker, that's all."

"Hooey!" Mirabelle snapped from the foot of his bed. "Your heart ain't no more wore out than mine. You've just been worrying too much over all them church responsibilities." She started fussing over him again, talking a mile a minute and cutting his meat loaf into little pieces. I backed slowly into the hall, waiting outside the door while Daddy Joe said his good-byes.

"Do you think they know about Ada Jane stealing the church money yet?" I asked him on the way to Tommy's room.

"It's hard to say, but if they don't, they'll find out soon enough. Nothing in Myron stays a secret for long."

The closer we got to Tommy's room, the faster my heart thumped. I worried again about what to say if he mentioned his dad. "Should I tell Tommy the truth?" I asked Daddy Joe.

He thought for a moment before answering. "I don't think it's necessary to tell him everything. Some things he'll figure out on his own."

I remembered how alone and scared Tommy had looked before his fall. "I feel so bad for him. He never says so, but I know he wants a dad real bad."

"Really?" Daddy Joe sounded surprised. "That should work out mighty fine, then, because I've always wanted two daughters and a son. I think Charlene would lend him over to us sometimes, don't you?"

I looked into Daddy Joe's serious eyes, and I knew he meant what he said. My face broke into a smile. I took his hand as we hurried down the corridor. I couldn't wait to see Tommy's expression when he saw the three of us.

We brought Tommy home on a Sunday. Before we left the hospital, he showed off for everyone on his new crutches, hobbling down the hall to get a drink from the water fountain. Of course, he started bragging then, telling everyone how the doctors and nurses hadn't ever seen anyone get the hang of crutches so quick. To tell the truth, the way he wobbled around, it didn't look to me like he had the hang of anything yet. I didn't say so, though.

All seven of us piled into the station wagon. Daddy Joe, Mama, and Aunt Charlene sat in the front. Tommy's cast took up the whole backseat, so Carla, Ernestine, and I got stuck in the very back of the car. Carla curled up on my lap with her hairless, one-armed Kimmy doll. I wrapped my arms around her and watched the summer sky spin by as we headed down the highway.

The last few weeks whirred through my head, starting with the day Daddy and Uncle Warren had robbed the bank. It was old news in Myron by now, but I knew everyone would start buzzing about it again once Daddy's trial began. It turned out he hadn't robbed any other banks like Ada Jane had said. There hadn't been a reward out for him, either. She'd just made all that stuff up. I knew she'd made up a ton of lies about my family, but it didn't bother me so much anymore. At least everyone knew it was her who stole the church money, not me and Tommy. She'd gotten into a ton of trouble, and I'd even seen her in the church kitchen, scrubbing the sink and counters alongside Mirabelle.

I sat back and thought about the letter I'd gotten from Daddy, postmarked from the Henderson County Jail. He hadn't been sent to the Pendleton Penitentiary yet; Mama said that would happen after the trial. In the letter Daddy told me how sorry he felt about everything. He said he'd made a big mistake by robbing the bank. I read it through a bunch of times, especially the part that said, "I love you, baby, and I want to get out of here real soon so I can make things right." I'd stuffed the letter in a box under my bed. I hadn't answered it yet.

I thought about everything during that car ride, but

mostly I just felt happy to be bringing Tommy home from the hospital. He had Tiger on his lap, and I had Carla on mine. My best friend was sitting beside me, and Daddy Joe and Mama were squashed together in the front seat, right where they belonged.

I'd almost dozed off when I heard the bell clanging at the railroad crossing. Our station wagon rolled to a stop, and I looked around, watching as the big black train engine roared around a curve in the tracks, its whistle blowing.

"Hey!" Tommy said. "That's weird."

"What's so weird about that? It's just a train." I poked his shoulder with the Kimmy doll and made a stupid face at him. Carla and Ernestine burst out laughing.

"It's Sunday, that's what's weird." Tommy grinned and poked me back with his crutch. "I thought you said the trains don't run on Sundays."

I felt my neck heat up.

Daddy Joe chuckled.

"Uh . . . I might've said that. I say a lot of stuff."

"Yep," Carla piped up. "You sure do say a lot of stuff. What about that time you said Daddy Joe was a you-know-what. That word I ain't supposed to say. Do you remember that, Billie?"

"Umm . . ." The heat slid up to my cheeks.

Everything got quiet for a couple of seconds before Daddy Joe started to laugh—a deep, rumbling laugh I never knew he had in him.

Mama and Aunt Charlene raised their eyebrows at me, acting shocked, but Daddy Joe laughed even more before he shook his head and said, "I've got to hand it to that girl of ours. She's not afraid to say what she thinks."

I grinned at him from the back of the car—a grin so wide it surely showed the gap between my front teeth.

Acknowledgments

Oh my. So many great people to thank; so little space. Tricky business for this word-a-holic, but here goes.

First, thank you to my wonderful agent, Wendy Schmalz, for believing in my book; for your smart advice; and for your warmth, wit, and friendship.

To Virginia Duncan, my publisher, and the fabulous Greenwillow staff, thank you for acquiring this book, and for the extraordinary care you took with the editing, cover, and design. You're the best!

A special, awestruck thank you to my editor, Martha Mihalick. What can I say, other than "Wow! How did Billie and I get so lucky?" Your attention to the heart of Billie's story, thought-provoking comments, and tireless editorial guidance certainly made Myron, Indiana, a more memorable place to visit.

Special thanks to Kelsey Johnson Defatte, for your willingness to read and reread and reread yet again, and for your great suggestions. Many thanks to everyone else who read this book in various stages, especially Marcy Skelton, Catherine Ipcizade, Linda Provence, Barry Eva, and Lois Toureen.

A huge thank you to Ann Likes: your friendship and support saw me through this whole process. Thanks so much to my fabulous cheerleader friends: Amy Call, Julia Karr, Laura Ley, and Maryhelen Silverthorn.

Many thanks to my brother and sister-in-law, Mike and Linda Kelsey, for your enthusiastic support and for the umpteen manuscript copies you provided. A lifetime of thanks to my aunt Ann, for your encouragement to pursue my dreams. And to my wonderful in-laws—the Walters—thanks so much for your well wishes and good cheer.

And finally, to the fabulous guys in my life: husband, Terry, and sons Christopher, Eric, and Max, thank you for being my most treasured audience. Without you, this couldn't have happened.

5/09